Stopping criminal activity wherever it happens. The agents at TCD are ready for anything.

More and more, federal law agencies have to mobilize to remote locations to address large-scale crime scenes and criminal activity—terror, hostage situations, kidnappings, shootings and the like. Because of the growing concerns and need for ever increasing response times to these criminal events, the Bureau created a specialized tech and tactical team, combining specialists from several active divisions—weapons, crime scene investigation, protection, negotiation, IT. Because they are a smaller unit, they are more nimble for rapid deployment and assistance to address various situations. This joint team of agents is known as the Tactical Crime Division.

48 HOUR LOCKDOWN

New York Times Bestselling Author

CARLA CASSIDY

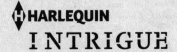

HARLEQUIN
INTRIGUE

Special thanks and acknowledgment are given to Carla Cassidy for her contribution to the Tactical Crime Division miniseries.

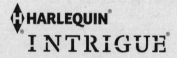

HARLEQUIN®
INTRIGUE®

ISBN-13: 978-1-335-13639-8

48 Hour Lockdown

Copyright © 2020 by Harlequin Books S.A.

This edition published by arrangement with Harlequin Books S.A.

For questions and comments about the quality of this book, please contact us at CustomerService@Harlequin.com.

Harlequin Enterprises ULC
22 Adelaide St. West, 40th Floor
Toronto, Ontario M5H 4E3, Canada
www.Harlequin.com

Printed in U.S.A.

Carla Cassidy is an award-winning, *New York Times* bestselling author who has written over 150 novels for Harlequin. In 1995, she won Best Silhouette Romance from *RT Book Reviews* for *Anything for Danny*. In 1998, she won a Career Achievement Award for Best Innovative Series from *RT Book Reviews*. Carla believes the only thing better than curling up with a good book to read is sitting down at the computer with a good story to write.

Books by Carla Cassidy

Harlequin Intrigue

48 Hour Lockdown

Desperate Strangers
Desperate Intentions
Desperate Measures

Scene of the Crime

Scene of the Crime: Bridgewater, Texas
Scene of the Crime: Bachelor Moon
Scene of the Crime: Widow Creek
Scene of the Crime: Mystic Lake
Scene of the Crime: Black Creek
Scene of the Crime: Deadman's Bluff
Scene of the Crime: Return to Bachelor Moon
Scene of the Crime: Return to Mystic Lake
Scene of the Crime: Baton Rouge
Scene of the Crime: Killer Cove
Scene of the Crime: Who Killed Shelly Sinclair?
Scene of the Crime: Means and Motive

Visit the Author Profile page at Harlequin.com.

CAST OF CHARACTERS

Evan Duran—Special Agent Duran is a hostage negotiator for the Tactical Crime Division, a specialized branch of the FBI.

Annalise Taylor—A teacher held hostage at a private school. She's also Evan's ex-lover. She'd broken his heart several years before, and now he holds her life in his hands.

Jacob Noble—Is he the leader of a charitable church or the dangerous leader of a cult?

Gretchen Noble—Jacob's wife, who is not afraid to abuse or kill. Will she kill Annalise before she can be freed?

Hendrick Maynard—Brilliant tech agent for the Tactical Crime Division. Will he be able to get the information Evan needs or will he be destroyed by old painful memories?

Walter Cummings—Chief of police in Asheville. Would his incompetence be the death of the hostages?

Prologue

"I've written a short essay on the board. Why don't you all rewrite it using our secret code?" Annalise Taylor said, and watched as the three girls seated before her focused on the computers in front of them.

Tanya Walton was thirteen years old, Emily Clariton was ten and Sadie Brubaker was nine. All of them wore blue trousers and white blouses with the Sandhurst School emblem embroidered in blue and green on the breast pocket.

The girls came from different areas of the United States, but they all shared a background of abject poverty, some abuse and a lack of opportunities. Until their bright minds brought them to this unusual private school built specifically for children like them, this place where their intelligence was both celebrated and nurtured.

As the girls continued to work, Annalise walked over to the window next to her desk and gazed outside. The school was located on fifteen acres on the outskirts of the charming town of Pearson, North Carolina.

From this vantage point, the view was absolutely breathtaking. The Blue Ridge Mountains surrounded the city. With more than a million acres of protected wilderness, there were plenty of hiking trails, secluded back roads and streams and waterfalls to explore. Right now the leaves on the trees were beginning to display the reds and oranges of autumn.

Annalise turned away from the vista and sat at her desk. She released a deep, weary sigh. It had been a long day. This class was not officially part of the curriculum, rather it was a sort of after-school club to feed the passions of these particular girls, who always looked forward to a little extra time to work and play on their computers.

A loud boom jolted her out of her mental haze, followed by another and another one. Annalise straightened. Was that…was that gunfire? What was going on? Gunfire! For a moment her brain froze in horror as the three girls screamed.

Lock the door! Push desks against it! The orders sounded in her head. That's what she was supposed to do. That's what she'd been trained to do in a situation like this.

Heart pounding, she jumped up from her seat and ran toward her classroom door. But before she could reach it, the door exploded inward and a large, burly man with a long gun stood on the threshold.

"Get down, get down," he screamed, and pointed to a wall with his automatic weapon. "All of you, sit down with your backs against the wall. Now."

"What's going on? What do you want?" Annalise asked the questions as she gathered her students close to her.

"Shut up and sit down," he demanded.

Terror ripped through Annalise as she moved the girls to the wall where they all slid down to sit on the floor. The girls were crying and she tried to comfort them…to shush them. The last thing she wanted was for their cries to irritate the man with the gun.

What did he want? Why was he here? Just then a tall, thin man came into the room. "I thought you told us nobody else would be here except these four," he said, and gestured toward Annalise and the girls.

"That was the information I had," the burly man replied.

"Well, now there's a dead security guard in the lobby, and two dead women in the main office." He shifted from one foot to the other. "Let's go. This has all gone sideways. We need to get the hell out of here."

Dear God. Annalise's heart beat so fast her stomach churned with nausea and an icy chill filled her veins. Bert was dead? The security guard with the great smile who loved to tell silly knock-knock jokes was gone? And which two women had been killed? Who had been in the office at the time of this… this attack?

What were these killers doing here? What did they want?

The sound of distant sirens pierced the air. The big man cursed loudly.

"We were supposed to get in and out of here before the cops showed up," the tall, thin man said with barely suppressed desperation in his voice.

"Too late for that now," the big man replied. He turned and pointed his gun at Annalise. She stiffened. Was he going to kill her, as well? Was he going to shoot her right now? Kill the girls? She put her arms around her students and tried to pull them all behind her.

More sirens whirred and whooped, coming closer and closer.

"Don't move," he snarled at them. He took the butt of his gun and busted out one of the windows. The sound of the shattering glass followed by a rapid burst of gunfire out the window made her realize just how dangerous this situation was.

The police were outside. She and her students were inside with murderous gunmen, and she couldn't imagine how this all was going to end.

Chapter One

Evan Duran sat at his kitchen table, dividing his attention between his television and his phone while he sipped his second cup of coffee. It was just a few minutes before ten on a Wednesday, his day off, and he'd slept later than usual.

Normally he would be already finished with his daily five-mile run, and in the office rather than waiting this late in the morning to even get started on his run.

He paused with his mug halfway between his mouth and the table when a news alert broke into the talk show that had been on.

HOSTAGE SITUATION IN NORTH CAROLINA. The bold words scrolled across the bottom of the screen. Evan grabbed his remote and turned up the sound as the female newscaster began the story.

"Breaking news out of the small town of Pearson, North Carolina, this morning. Last night at approximately five o'clock armed men burst into the Sandhurst School. According to the latest reports, there has already been confirmed fatalities and the hostages include teachers and students. The names of the children are being withheld, but the staff inside include Annalise Taylor and Belinda Baker..."

Evan stared at the television as he slowly put down his mug. Annalise? A hostage in a school in Pearson, North Carolina? Last he knew, she was working at an elite private college in Missouri.

It wasn't necessarily his personal history with Annalise that pulled him up from his chair and set him in motion. If there was an ongoing hostage situation, Evan needed to get there to help.

He went into his master bedroom, quickly changing out of his running clothes and into a white button-down shirt and a pair of black pants. He grabbed his jacket with TCD—Tactical Crime Division—stenciled on the back and headed for the front door.

Annalise. A vision of her exploded in his head. For two years they'd been a couple. He'd just assumed eventually they'd marry. Instead, almost three years ago she had left him. She'd broken it off with him in a text message.

He couldn't think about all the emotions thoughts of her threatened to evoke. Right now there was a hostage situation.

When it came to hostage negotiation, nobody was better than him. A fact. Not conceit.

Adrenaline rocked through Evan minutes later as he drove toward Knoxville, Tennessee, to Old City, where the TCD offices were located. While the FBI's headquarters were in DC, there were field offices all over the country.

The Tactical Crime Division was a specialized tech and tactical unit combining skilled professionals from several active divisions. Because they were smaller units they were more nimble for rapid deployment and could quickly proffer assistance to address various situations—especially in more rural areas without a large police force.

As he drove he made a few phone calls, and he finally pulled up in front of the nondescript brick building where TCD's offices were located. He parked, got out of his car and hurried inside. As he strode down the hallway toward the main meeting room, he could hear Director Jill Pembrook apparently still conducting the morning meeting.

The main conference room was the heart of the office. It was where assignments were handed out and situations were brainstormed. The agents sat at a long, highly glossed wooden table. On one wall was an oversize FBI logo, and opposite that was the TCD emblem. A large, digital flat screen was mounted on the far side of the room, and a tablet lay at the head of the table.

Evan burst through the door. Director Jill Pembrook looked at him in surprise. "Agent Duran, how nice of you to join us on your day off."

The director was an attractive, stylish woman of substance with cropped steel gray hair and a penchant for dark, custom-tailored suits.

She'd been with the FBI for over forty years, and

she was definitely a force to be reckoned with. Her blue eyes could be warm and friendly or they could frost a puddle of water into a sheet of ice.

"I just saw the news out of Pearson," he stated. "I need to get there… It's Annalise."

There was a collective groan from some of the other agents. Evan ignored it. "I'll need you to arrange a plane to be ready for takeoff. Also, I'll need Hendrick's help on this. And I'm taking Agents Brennan and Lathrop with me."

"Call off the SEAL team, Duran is on the case, everyone," "Agent at Large" Kane Bradshaw murmured as the three men headed for the door.

Evan ignored him. While he liked Kane okay, there were times in the past they had butted heads when Kane could sometimes be a bit of an arrogant jerk. Director Pembrook though tolerated his glib attitude. And while Kane had no official rank as an agent with the bureau, he had an extensive background with deep black ops.

Hendrick Maynard, the tech guru nodded. "You got it," he answered without hesitation. "Heading to my desk now. I'll send you any relevant info ASAP."

The director narrowed her eyes, and Evan felt the frost radiating from her. "Agent Duran, you are way out of line." She paused and continued to hold his gaze. "Ten minutes ago North Carolina state officials called for federal help…" She paused and he was wondering if he should offer to submit his resignation. "You will also take Special Agent Rogers along with the others. This is an all hands on deck situation. Rowan as usual will accompany you and provide team support."

Rowan Cooper, an attractive woman with long dark hair who worked as a liaison between the local police departments and the TCD team members, also rose and followed the men out the door. She accompanied any crew that deployed to a different location. Her specialty was smoothing over any personality difference or turf wars among different law enforcement units on scene. But her main responsibility was arranging overnight accommodations and making sure the agents had what they needed in order to remain focused on the task at hand.

"Yes, ma'am," he replied to the director. He knew he'd overstepped boundaries by barging in, but he'd felt the need to act immediately when he'd heard about the situation… About Annalise…

"Plane leaves in twenty minutes. Now go," Director Pembrook said. To him she added, "Duran… don't pull this kind of stunt again."

Evan would have offered to quit *after* the assignment if he met any resistance from the director to him heading up the detail due to his personal connection to Annalise. Nothing was going to keep him from negotiating this hostage situation.

"Never," Evan replied before turning to leave.

The team headed for the locker rooms where the agents had go bags of clothing and personal items since they often headed out on a moment's notice. Rowan was equally prepared for the mission. Usually she would precede the agents to any given location when assignments were handed out, but in this case there was no time.

He knew he was working with the best team and that they would resolve the hostage situation no matter what. Special Agent Davis Rogers was a former army ranger and had been with TCD for only three years, but he was a good fit. He excelled at tricky reconnaissance, among other things.

Agents Nick Brennan and Daniel Lathrop were both not only easy to get along with, but they also possessed specific skills that would make them assets.

The four of them, along with the local law enforcement officials, had to work together to end the standoff with nobody else getting hurt—or worse.

By the time he and the other agents boarded the plane, Hendrick had already sent them all an email with information about the school, along with blueprints of the building.

The school had been established five years earlier by Regina Sandhurst, the CEO of a large tech company who had grown up in the area and wanted to give back. She believed the youth of the nation was a resource to nurture and foster.

She also believed children from disadvantaged communities needed to be fostered, and therefore the year-round school offered full scholarships to underprivileged girls who made up the student body.

The twenty-six students lived on the stately campus, and most were between the ages of nine and fourteen. Dr. Olivia Wright was the principal, and six teachers provided the daily curriculum. There was also a cleaning and cooking staff and six women who were live-in residents and looked after the students.

Evan read carefully over the information. High risk negotiation was what he did, but the stakes were always higher when children were involved. And Annalise...

Her name whispered through his head, but he shoved any thoughts of her away. He had a job to do, and it didn't matter who was being held in the school; he intended to get everyone out alive and well.

"According to Hendrick, nobody has learned what the hostage takers want." Evan broke the silence that had overtaken everyone in the plane.

"What would these people want to achieve by invading a school?" Nick asked.

"I don't have a clue," Evan replied. "According to Hendrick's notes, the school doesn't hold large amounts of cash on-site."

"Maybe they are planning to ransom off the kids," Daniel said.

"To who?" Evan countered as he continued to read the brief. "It seems most of these kids come from impoverished households." He looked up. "Let's hope by the time we touch down the local authorities will have more information for us. This situation has already gone on for a full night."

They all fell silent once again. With each minute that ticked by, the tension in the plane increased.

He knew all the agents were feeling the pressure of getting this right, but ultimately as the negotiator, the weight of this situation was on his shoulders.

While there were a lot of tried and true ways to deal with a hostage taker, much of his strategy would ultimately come down to instinct as each situation was different. There was no way to prepare for what was ahead of him. He just had to be ready for anything and rely on his extensive training.

By the time the plane landed, he was pumped and ready to get to the scene as quickly as possible. They loaded into a waiting van and took off for the scene of the crime.

"Hendrick sent me some information about the Pearson chief of police," Rowan said from the front seat.

She was young for an agent, only in her early twenties. Rowan was skilled in dealing with all levels of police personnel. She was a real asset when it came to coordinating the team with local law enforcement and also skilled at clearing red tape for the agents.

"Walter Cummings has been chief of police here for the past seven years. According to the locals, he's a bit of a blowhard and showman but runs his department with an iron fist," Rowan said.

"I'm sure you'll manage him just fine," Evan said. "We're going to need the support of all the local police."

He sat up straighter in his seat as he saw the two brick buildings in the distance. The larger one housed dorms for the residents. The smaller one held the classrooms the students attended every day—even on weekends for half days—and that was where the armed men had burst in and taken hostages.

In front of the school was a wide paved driveway. The relatively small parking lot was filled with a fleet of first responder vehicles and personnel as well as what appeared to be a large onlooker presence. Too many civilians for Evan's comfort level.

"It looks like a cluster—" Davis started to say.

The van came to a halt. "Let's get this under control," Evan said as they all exited the unmarked vehicle.

It took Evan and Rowan several minutes to work their way through the crowd and finally locate Chief Walter Cummings. He was a squat, barrel-chested man with salt-and-pepper hair and broken blood vessels across his nose and cheeks.

"Chief Cummings?" Rowan said, and held out her hand. "Rowan Cooper with the TCD. This is Special Agent Evan Duran, TCD's top hostage negotiator."

He shook Rowan's hand first, then Evan's, using a hard, viselike grip that Evan assumed was meant to be intimidating. It didn't work. "I'd say I'm glad to see you folks here, but I'll be honest. This is a matter I thought we could handle. But you know the state boys were worried about regulations—"

"The last thing we want to do is step on anyone's toes," Rowan replied smoothly. "We all have one goal in mind, right? We need to get the hostages

out safe and sound and put the hostage takers behind bars."

"I'll need details about the hostages inside the
building," Evan said, cutting to the chase.

The chief rocked back on his heels. "The principal, two teachers and four students, along with a
security guard."

"Do you know how many hostage takers are in
there?" Evan asked.

"No, I don't," he replied. "We've tried to call the
main office, but nobody from the inside is talking
to let us know what's going on in there. We know
the security guard is dead, but we aren't sure who
else might be." The chief grimaced. "Bert Epstein
was a personal friend of mine. His body is there in
the front doorway."

"I'm sorry you lost your friend," Evan replied,
but did not have time for more than the cursory con-
dolence. "You have a number for a phone inside the
school?" Evan didn't remember whether Hendrick
had sent a phone number or not.

Walter nodded and gave it to him. "It's the only
number I have. It rings in the office."

"And you have no idea who the armed men are
or what they want?" Evan asked. This situation had
already been going on for almost twenty-four hours,
and Chief Cummings didn't know anything? Was
the man just that incompetent?

Walter shrugged. "No clue."

Evan looked toward the other building on the
property. "I understand that is where all the stu-

dents live. I'm assuming you have armed guards at the door and the place is on lockdown?"

"Affirmative," the chief replied.

"Who are all these people?" Evan asked, and swept one of his arms toward the onlookers. "There seems to be a lot of civilians just standing around." They were people who not only contributed to the chaos of the active scene but also stood a chance of taking a bullet if things went sideways. They needed to be moved out of the area immediately.

"Some of them are teachers who work at the school and are concerned for the people who are inside. They're also townsfolk interested in what's going on. We don't usually have a situation like this," Chief Cummings explained.

"We need to move them all out of here as quickly as possible," Evan said. He looked at Rowan. "Maybe you could help the chief get some of his men together to get any civilians safely off the premises."

"Are you sure you don't need any of my input right now on how you're going to handle this?" the chief asked.

"Not at this moment," Evan replied. Right now more than anything he hoped to make contact with somebody inside. He wouldn't know how to negotiate the release of the hostages without gaining some kind of information about the people who were holding them. The most important thing was to find out why they were in the school and what they wanted in order to release the hostages unharmed.

He stared at the school. How many people were

actually dead inside? Was it possible Annalise was one of the them? He could see a man's body lying prone in the front doorway. That would be the security guard Chief Cummings had mentioned.

His chest tightened. The stakes were high. If these men had already killed people, then they had nothing to lose and there was no assurance they wouldn't kill more.

IT HAD BEEN a night of hell. Throughout the long hours of darkness, men had been in and out of the room, peeking out the window and cursing. The girls had whimpered and cried, and Annalise had also heard the cries and moans of fellow teacher Belinda Baker and another student coming from the room across the hall.

Finally the girls had all fallen into an exhausted sleep, and even Annalise had managed to catch an hour or two of dreamless sleep.

But the day was upon them, a day of fear and uncertainty. "The girls need to use the restroom again," she said to the burly man who seemed to be in charge of everything. She'd heard several of the other men call him Jacob.

He whirled around from his position on a chair just to the side of the broken window and scowled at her, as if she were personally responsible for nature's call.

"Gretchen," he bellowed.

Annalise sat up straighter. Gretchen? There was a woman here with all the men? A tiny bit of hope surged inside her. Maybe she could talk a woman into letting the children go.

A woman with grayish hair fashioned into two long braids strode into the room. She carried a pistol and smiled at Jacob. "Hey, baby, did you call for me?"

"Yeah, they have to go to the bathroom. You want to take them?"

"Sure," she replied. She turned to Annalise and the children. "Up," she said curtly. "Let's go."

Gretchen was a thin older woman with light blue eyes and a careworn face. Whether she could reason with this woman was an unknown. Nonetheless, right now it felt good to get up and stretch after sitting for so long, but the situation also still felt volatile and dangerous.

The restroom was right outside the classroom and to the left. Annalise wanted to check in on Belinda and whoever might be with the fellow teacher in the room across the way, but she got no opportunity as Gretchen led them directly to the girls' restroom.

She stood just outside the door as Annalise and the girls went inside. Alone with the girls, she wiped away tears and told them she would do whatever possible to keep them safe. "We all just have to be brave," she said.

As the girls were washing their hands, Annalise stepped out where Gretchen awaited. "Is there any way I can appeal to you to let the children go?" she said. "You'll all still have me as a hostage, but this is no place for children."

Gretchen shrugged. "Sorry. My husband is in charge of this operation and he makes the rules."

"Your husband?"

"Jacob." Gretchen's chin shot up in obvious pride. "He's the leader of the Brotherhood of Jacob, and all of us who are here believe in the path he has us on."

"A path of crime and murder?" The words snapped out of Annalise with a hint of the anger that had been festering inside her since this all began.

Gretchen stepped closer to Annalise and without warning slapped her hard. Annalise immediately raised her hand to her burning cheek as her eyes began to water. "Have some respect," Gretchen snarled.

Anger swelled up in Annalise, but she had to swallow hard against it as at that moment the girls came out of the bathroom. Besides, Gretchen had a gun and Annalise had no idea if the woman would actually use it or not. As they once again took their positions against the wall, Annalise's cheek still burned.

"Everything all right?" Jacob asked.

"Everything is fine. I just had to give the teacher a lesson in respect," Gretchen replied. The woman looked at Annalise with narrowed eyes. "Let's hope she's a fast study."

Moments later when Gretchen had left the room, Annalise glanced at the girls. Although Tanya and Emily continued to cry, it was Sadie who worried Annalise the most.

Sadie's background not only included poverty, she had also been physically and emotionally abused by her mother, a young drug addict hooked on heroin and bad men.

When Sadie had first come to the school, she had been a solemn, closed-off child who flinched each time she made a mistake. Over the past few months, Sadie had shared a lot of feelings and emotions with Annalise, creating a special bond between teacher and student.

It had been Annalise's greatest joy to watch the little girl blossom and become a precocious, giggling nine-year-old who loved hugs and reveled in her own accomplishments. Despite being the youngest, she was the brightest of the three, but at the moment none of that beautiful light shone from her eyes.

Now, she was stone-faced, her big blue eyes holding a blankness that broke Annalise's heart. What damage was this doing to her? To all the girls?

"Please let the children go," she said to Jacob. "You'll still have me as a hostage. Just let the children go."

"That's not going to happen so just shut up about it," he replied, and raked a hand through his black hair.

"What's the Brotherhood of Jacob?" she asked. She was aware that her cell phone was plugged into an outlet behind the desk and on a shelf half-hidden by puzzle books. Thankfully the ringer and notifications were turned off. So far she hadn't had a chance to get to it, but if she did get a chance she would call out and at least be able to tell the police who these people were and what they wanted. All she needed was to find out exactly why they were here and what they did want.

"We are the Brotherhood of Jacob," Jacob replied. "We have a plan, and we intend to see it through to the end."

"Surely your plan didn't include being trapped inside this building that by now is surrounded by squads of law enforcement officers. What is it you want? Why did you come here in the first place?"

"You don't need to know anything, so just shut your trap and don't bother me." He turned back toward the window.

In the relative quiet of the building, she could hear low moans coming from across the hallway and a phone ringing. The phone had to be the one in the main office as that was the only phone in the building.

The moans worried her. She was sure it had to be Belinda, and she had to be hurt to be moaning so much. Was anything being done to help her? Who else was in that classroom with her?

Jacob turned to look at her once again. "Is there any food in this place?"

"The only thing is a snack closet in the hallway. Would you please see to it that these girls get something to eat? I'm sure they're all hungry."

The snack closet was supplied with relatively healthy food like fruit chews and prepackaged apple slices and baked goods. Granola bars were usually replenished daily. There were also some juice packs, bags of chips and candy bars.

In this situation if the girls had pretzels for breakfast, she didn't care, as long as they got something to eat.

"I thought this was all a really bad dream," Tanya whispered.

"Me, too," Emily replied.

"We're all okay. Mr. Jacob has said he'll give you something to eat in just a little while," Annalise said softly. "What about you, Sadie? Are you hungry?"

Sadie grabbed the ends of her long blond hair and began to twirl them, a gesture Annalise recognized as an old, self-soothing action. Her blue eyes stared at Annalise as she shook her head negatively.

"Jacob, won't you please let the girls go?"

"They aren't going anywhere. What do you think is keeping the cops from storming this building right now? These girls are our golden ticket out of here."

Gretchen came back into the room. "People are complaining about being hungry."

Jacob told her about the food closet. "See to it that you throw something to these girls, too."

"Thank you, Mr. Jacob," Sadie said, surprising Annalise. Apparently Sadie was paying far more attention to what was going on around her than Annalise had initially believed.

Jacob grunted. Minutes later Gretchen returned with three packages of minimuffins. She tossed one to each of the girls. "What about Miss Annalise?" Sadie asked.

"She'll be fine," Gretchen said, her blue eyes cold as she gazed at Annalise.

Sadie frowned and looked at Annalise. "I'll share with you, Miss Annalise."

"It's okay, honey. You go ahead and eat it. I'm not hungry right now." Annalise only wanted these sweet, wonderful girls out of here. She'd do anything to get them to safety.

The morning hours crept by slowly. What did these people, these Brotherhood of Jacob members, want and how did they believe they would ever be able to somehow walk away from all this? According to what she'd heard, there were already three dead people. All she could hope for was that the girls who depended on her would get out of this safely.

The tall, thin man, named Thomas, came into the room. He'd been in and out several times throughout the night. "Jacob, some of our people are still complaining about that ringing phone," he said.

Jacob released a breath that was clearly exasperation. "Sounds like I've got a lot of whiners and complainers with me. Next thing you know you'll all be screaming like a bunch of pathetic women, and you know how much I hate pathetic women."

"Jacob, we all agreed to your original plan, but none of us signed up to get trapped inside this building for an endless amount of time," Thomas replied.

"Do you doubt our mission?" Jacob's voice thundered, and his eyes filled with a fiery glint. "Do you doubt that we are the chosen ones to follow through on this mission? Do you all doubt me?"

"Of course not." Thomas took a couple of steps backward, as if moved there by the sheer force of Jacob's voice and fierceness. "We all believe in this… we believe in you, but how long before you start negotiating our way out of this mess?"

Jacob rose from his chair, his features twisted with anger. "I'll negotiate when I think the time is right." He turned around and shot off his gun through the window. The three short blasts caused Annalise to jump and the girls to scream.

He turned and faced them. "Shut up! Stop that screaming."

Annalise pulled the girls closer to her and tried to shush them. Fear torched through her. The man was obviously volatile and unpredictable. Thankfully no return fire came from the outside.

"Stop calling that phone," Jacob yelled out the window. "If you don't stop, I'm going to start throwing out the bodies of dead little girls."

An icy chill filled Annalise. Would he really follow through on the threat? It was obvious the phone had been ringing because somebody on the outside was trying to make contact. The ringing stopped.

"How are you going to get out of here if you don't talk to anyone from the outside?" Annalise asked in frustration. "And why are you here? What do you want?"

"Nobody is talking to you, so you need to shut up and mind your own business," Jacob growled at her. "Besides, the longer they get nervous out there, the more apt they are to bargain with me."

"You know no money is kept here and most of the students come from impoverished families." There was no way the students could be exchanged for a large sum of money.

"Don't you worry about what I know," Jacob retorted.

"I'm speaking to the people in the school building. I'm Special Agent Evan Duran with the Tactical Crimes Division of the FBI," a deep voice said from a bullhorn outside.

Annalise's heart seemed to stop beating for a wild moment. *Evan...?* Evan was here? Suddenly her head was filled with sweeping memories...memories of passion and laughter, of love and of loss.

There had been a time when he'd been the love of her life—her endgame, she thought. He now held her life in his hands. She just hoped he took better care of it than she had with his heart.

Chapter Two

The gunfire coming out of the school window definitely had everyone on the outside scrambling for cover, but the good news was somebody had yelled out the window and hopefully that meant the people inside were ready to engage.

The other good news was all the civilians had been moved away from the scene, and Evan had everything in place that he needed.

He now held the bullhorn in his hand, although he stood behind a patrol car in case more bullets flew out the window and he needed to take cover.

He had considered turning off the electricity to the building to make things more uncomfortable for the hostage takers, but ultimately had decided against it considering there were children involved. They had kept the water on for the same reason.

Right now he was angry—beyond angry—that apparently somebody had been calling the school's office over and over again and that somebody had not been him, nor had they been working under his direct orders. He had a sneaking suspicion who it had been.

He turned to Nick, who was standing beside him. "Do me a favor. Find the chief of police and bring him to me."

"On it." Nick left and Evan turned his attention back at the school. The first thing he wanted to address with the hostage takers was the wounded and dead. But he hadn't had a chance to do anything before shots had been fired out of the window, along with the dire warning about throwing out bodies.

Regina Sandhurst had been out of town when this all went down, but she was expected to arrive sometime late this afternoon. Hopefully she would have some useful information for them.

"You wanted to see me?" The police chief's voice boomed from behind Evan.

He turned to face him. The chief was definitely beginning to look worse for wear. Lines of exhaustion were etched across his broad forehead, and his uniform was a wrinkled mess. He had a stain on the front of his shirt and what appeared to be crumbs from a pastry on his fingers. Rowan stood just behind him, obviously ready to smooth any ruffled feathers that might—would—occur.

Rowan knew Evan very well. He didn't suffer fools gladly and he often didn't mince words, especially when lives were on the line.

"Have you been the one calling the school phone over and over again?" Evan asked.

"Yes. I was hoping to open up a line of conversation," he replied.

"They just threatened to throw out a dead child if the ringing doesn't stop," Evan replied, and tried to tamp down his anger. "You were working at cross-purposes with me. We can't do that. Do not interfere without talking to my team first. There can only be one lead in this situation, and right now I'm it."

The chief frowned, and it was obvious he didn't like what Evan had to say. "I'm still the chief of police around here," he began.

Rowan placed a hand on the chief's shoulder. "We certainly respect your position," she said smoothly. "Our goal is like yours…to get the hostages out safe and sound and the killers behind bars. Agent Duran is highly trained in negotiation, and we need to give him a chance to do his job."

The chief grunted and then raked a hand through his hair. "If you're sure you've got this for now, I believe I'll take off. I'll go home. It was a long night."

It was the man's way of acquiescing to Evan without losing face. "Hopefully when you get back this will all be over and the hostages will be safe," Evan replied. Things would definitely go smoother if the chief was off-site and Evan didn't have to worry about him mucking things up.

To that end Evan raised the bullhorn to his mouth once again. "I'm talking to the men in the school. Will you tell me who I'm speaking with?"

"You're speaking to the man in charge." A deep voice boomed out one of the broken windows.

Evan squinted in an effort to get a visual of the person speaking, but the man kept his body just out of sight. Daniel was a skilled sniper, and Evan knew he was already looking for a place to set up where he would have a kill shot if necessary.

"Give me your name," Evan yelled back.

"I'll tell you when you need to know who I am," the man yelled back.

"Okay. Look, I'm sure you didn't plan on or want to be in the situation you're in right now. I'd like to understand your position better. Could you tell me why you're here?"

"I'm not ready to have a conversation right now."

"I'm sure we can work something out here as long as none of the hostages are harmed. Right now I'd like for you to release anyone who needs medical help." Evan not only wanted anyone who was hurt to be released, but once that was done he needed to get the deceased out of that building.

"Why don't you back up all your officers as a show of good faith?" the gruff voice yelled from the window.

"I'd like to do that for you, but before I do could you let us get to the wounded?" Evan asked.

"We have nothing to talk about." Gunfire punctuated the man's sentence.

Evan cursed and ducked back behind the patrol car. "At least you got somebody talking to you," Davis said as he crouched next to Evan.

"It didn't do much to move things forward, but it did break the ice." Evan sighed in frustration. "I really wish we could get a name of the leader inside. With a little information on him, I might know what buttons to push. As it is, I'm working completely blind."

Davis clapped him on the back. "You'll get this right, Evan. You've gotten it right a hundred times before."

Evan nodded even as his frustration grew. There just wasn't enough information. The FBI had five negotiation techniques that had more often than not worked for Evan in past situations.

The first step was to listen to their side of things and make them aware he was listening. Unfortunately, so far they weren't really talking to Evan.

The next step was to show empathy, to let them know Evan had an understanding of where they were coming from and how they felt.

Then it was important to establish a rapport that would get them to start to trust him. Once he'd established that trust, then they could work on the problem together and he'd recommend a course of action.

Finally, if all those steps were followed, the last step was a behavioral change on their part, a change that would hopefully have them surrender.

Unfortunately, the process didn't work well if any of the steps were skipped, and right now he couldn't even get past the first step.

"Agent Duran?" He turned at the sound of an unfamiliar female voice. Two older women approached him. "I'm Susan DeKalb and this is Lydia McGraw," the older of the two began.

"You shouldn't be here," Evan said. Taking Susan's elbow, he walked her back behind the line of fire. "Now, what can I do for you?" He frowned, not liking the fact that the two had gotten past the police officers who were supposed to be keeping unauthorized people out of this area.

"We're both teachers and we're here with another teacher, Candice Winsky. We were wondering what, if anything, we can do to help."

"Do you have any idea who the people are who stormed the school?" he asked.

"None of us have a clue," Susan said. "We were wondering what you know about this." She grabbed Evan's forearm, desperation in her light brown eyes. "Do you know who is inside? Has anyone told you what this is all about?" She dropped her hold on his arm.

"Not at this point. Has anyone interviewed you all yet?"

"No, nobody has talked to us about any of this," Susan replied.

Once again Evan was struck by how little had been done before his arrival to secure the scene and gather information. "The best thing you can all do right now is stay behind the lines." He gestured to Nick. "This is Agent Brennan. I'd like him to interview you all. Nick, will you take care of this for me?"

"Absolutely."

As Nick led the women to a van set up specifically for interviews, Evan returned to his position
by the patrol car. Not only should all of the teachers be interviewed, but also everyone who worked at
the school. He'd just assumed that Chief Cummings
had already begun that process, but it was obvious
Evan needed to set that up with his own people. He
also needed to find out who made deliveries to the
school and have those people interviewed. Given
that the local law officers probably did little more
than handle traffic violations, the current situation
was likely more extreme than they had ever handled,
and they were understandably in over their heads.

He turned and stared at the building, gathering
his thoughts. He had to get this right. If he screwed
this up, people would die. Children were in danger.

The name of another little girl flew through his
head. Maria. A deep, familiar pain ripped through
him. She had been his younger sister, and he somehow felt that in saving the children in the school, it
might assuage some of the guilt he carried for not
being able to save Maria.

HENDRICK MAYNARD SAT in his office at TCD headquarters with his feet up on his desk and his chair
reared back. Mounted on the wall straight ahead
were half a dozen monitors, and three state-of-the-
art computers sat on the desk before him.

The wall to his left held two large posters, despite being against regulations, of his favorite bands
frozen in performance. This little office was his

space—his world—and he had to confess he liked to color outside the lines.

He'd been waiting for something…anything he could get that would help the situation in Pearson. But despite surfing the web all night long, he'd found absolutely nothing useful. Now it was up to Evan to get him something to sink his teeth into, something he could do to help the victims.

He hated that children were involved. He hated any crimes that were perpetrated against innocent kids. He personally knew what it was like to be a kid and to be helpless in a bad situation. He knew what it was like to look to adults for help and for none to be forthcoming.

He grabbed the energy drink can on the desk and took a drink. The last thing he wanted to do was fall back into old and painful memories that would help nobody.

Shifting positions in his chair, he continued to check the monitors for any sign of Evan or any of the other agents in Pearson. He knew they had a mobile van set up there with a computer directly linked to him.

Unfortunately, the four security cameras on the campus had been destroyed and now weren't recording anything. He'd checked the images right before they had stopped working, and three of them had shown nothing amiss until they'd malfunctioned. He assumed those cameras had probably been shot out from a distance.

The fourth camera had shown a black panel van

approaching the school's back door. Before anyone got out of the van, that camera had been shot out, as well.

During the night another agent had come into the office to spell him, but Hendrick had refused to relinquish his position at the computers. Evan couldn't take a break, and so neither would Hendrick. He was Evan's ride or die agent on this particular case.

Hendrick looked at Evan like the big brother he'd never had. The two men had shared many conversations, deep conversations that had touched on personal things. Evan was the only person with whom Hendrick had shared the true horror of the first ten years of his life. Evan was definitely more like family to him.

"Hey, how about some lunch? For some reason Director Pembrook thinks you might need to eat," Will Simpson said as he came into the office. Will worked as a civilian employee for TCD. He carried a tray from the cafeteria with him. "Today's special is baked pasta with garlic toast and an apple."

"Ah, ziti…the food of the gods," Hendrick replied.

Will laughed. Hendrick took the tray from him. "Thanks, man."

"Anything breaking?" Will asked, and gestured toward the computers.

"Not a damned thing. I'm thinking about doing my 'catch a perp' dance around the room except it requires a good deal of nudity and incense."

Will laughed again and shook his head. "Nothing you could do would ever surprise me, Hendrick."

"Whatever is good for the cause, man…right?"

"Right," Will replied with a wide grin. "I'll just get out of here and let you eat."

Minutes later, as Hendrick ate his meal and kept his eyes on the monitors, he marveled at where his life had taken him. He'd never really thought about being an FBI agent. He'd never thought of being any kind of law enforcement official while growing up.

When he'd been attending Harvard on a full scholarship, he'd just assumed he'd graduate with a degree in computer sciences and then maybe start his own business.

But halfway through his junior year, exceeding his teachers' expectations but bored to death with the curriculum, he'd dropped out.

He'd had no idea what he was going to do. He'd considered backpacking in Europe for a while, but that felt way too clichéd. He'd finally settled for a job with an IT company.

For the next three months, he was once again bored out of his mind. He spent his days doing his job and collecting a sizable paycheck, then at night he wrote code for all kinds of programs just to challenge himself.

When a couple of FBI agents had shown up at his front door late one evening, his first thought was that he was going to be arrested. He sometimes broke through firewalls on the internet. The bigger the company the larger the thrill. He did this just to see if he could, and he'd believed he was busted.

Instead of arresting him, to his surprise, the FBI had offered him a job. He'd landed at the TCD five years ago when he'd turned twenty-one years old. He'd never looked back.

He'd immediately felt at home here. He liked and admired the men and women who were his co-workers, but more important he felt like he'd finally found a real purpose in life. He liked using his brain and his skills for all the right reasons. He liked helping the other agents catch the criminals.

"Come on, Evan," he whispered toward the blank monitor. "Get me something."

ONE HOUR BLENDED into another and another as the girls and Annalise remained seated against the wall. Tanya and Emily napped off and on, but Sadie remained wide-awake.

"Are we going to die?" she whispered to Annalise.

"No, honey, we're going to be fine. We just need to be strong right now. Have you heard the man on the loudspeaker outside?" Sadie nodded. "He'll make sure we're all okay."

Sadie finally settled against Annalise's side and dozed off. Annalise wished she felt as confident as she hoped her words had sounded to Sadie.

Evan was a skilled negotiator, but he couldn't talk rationally and work out some sort of compromise with a madman. Evan was good, but Jacob definitely looked and acted like a crazy person, and his wife Gretchen was even worse.

Evan had been talking to Jacob over the bullhorn about every fifteen minutes, but Jacob wasn't responding. He just sat in the chair to the side of the broken window and stared out. Occasionally one of the other men or Gretchen would come in to whisper with Jacob.

It was after one man left the room that Jacob stood and stretched. "I'm going to leave you alone right now, but if you try to do anything to get away or help the girls escape, I'll shoot you without hesitation. Got it?" His dark eyes burned into hers.

She held his cold gaze and nodded. A shudder threatened to work through her as he stared at her for another long terrifying moment before he finally left the classroom.

What did he expect her to do? Stuff each of the traumatized girls out of the broken window? That would be far too dangerous. It was possible the children might be mistaken for the killers and hurt or even shot by the phalanx of armed police outside. Besides, she had no idea who might be watching out other school windows and could possibly shoot them all in the back as they tried to run for safety. No, it was far too risky.

However, with nobody watching them there were two things she needed to do. She wanted to get her phone and try to reach police or someone on the outside, and she needed to check on Belinda.

The minute Jacob left, she sprang into action. She

raced across the room, grabbed her cell phone and hit 911. "I'm a hostage in the Sandhurst School in North Carolina," she said when the call connected, speaking as quickly and as quietly as she could. "My name is Annalise Taylor, and I'm here with three students in room 106 at the Sandhurst School. We're being held by a group called the Brotherhood of Jacob. They've killed three people and wounded at least one more." She then gave her phone number and hung up.

She quickly hung up, replaced her phone, then ran across the room to the doorway. She peeked out. Seeing nobody, and hearing Jacob's voice coming from another room up the hallway, she raced across to the classroom.

Belinda Baker, the math teacher, was slumped against the wall, her bloody hands holding a wound in her stomach. Next to her was ten-year-old Amanda Ingraham, another student who looked positively terrified.

"Belinda—" Annalise fell to the floor next to her fellow teacher "—how bad is it?"

"I'm not sure, but it's definitely painful." The words came in short gasps. "Annalise, you need to take care of Amanda…promise me."

"I promise, but I'm going to try to get you out of here so you can get some medical attention."

Belinda released a small laugh that transformed into a deep sob. "Good luck with that. They left me in here to die. Do they know you're in here talking to me?"

"No. Jacob left the room, so I sneaked over here."

Belinda's brown eyes widened. "Annalise, go before you get caught. You need to stay safe so you can take care of the children. Please…just go."

Annalise knew she was right, but she hated to leave the wounded woman without being able to help her in some way. She got up and ran to the closet where most teachers kept a first-aid kit. She found the metal box on the top shelf, pulled it down and then quickly ran back to Belinda's side.

Tears blurred her vision as she opened it and stared down at the contents. Bandages, antibacterial ointment, adhesive tape…things for small wounds and scrapes. There was absolutely nothing in there that could help a woman who had been shot in the stomach.

"Go, Annalise," Belinda said. "Go before you get caught."

Reluctantly she rose and shot back across the hall and slid back into her place against the wall just moments before Jacob walked back in.

Her heart pounded a million beats a minute, making her feel half-nauseous. Had her phone message been received? She'd been so frantic to get the information out she hadn't given the 911 operator a chance to say anything. Would the message find its way to Evan?

And what about Belinda? She had to do something to get the woman help. "Jacob, I know there's somebody wounded across the hall. We can hear her moans. Won't you please let her go so she can get medical treatment?"

"You need to mind your own business," he replied tersely. "I'm not letting anyone go, and I don't want you talking to me about it again."

Annalise sighed in frustration. She sat up a little straighter as two men she hadn't seen before came into the room. How many of them were there?

The men spoke in low tones, and she couldn't hear any of the conversation. Were they plotting something? Her blood chilled as one of the men turned and looked at the girls.

Were they planning on using the girls as human shields to escape from here? Worse, were they here to take the girls for some sort of human trafficking?

No, surely not. Unfortunate as it was, there were much easier ways to grab little children off the streets. This was far too big a scheme. They were after something else, but what?

She tried to stop her imagination from running wild with horrible scenarios, but it was difficult not to think of terrible things in the position they were in and considering the man who was in charge.

One of the men left the room while the second man remained. Sadie awakened, and before Annalise could stop her, she jumped to her feet and walked over to Jacob. "Did I say that you could get up?" he half snarled at her.

"No, but I wanted to ask you if you would please get us something else to eat. My belly has been growling and growling because I'm so hungry. And what about Miss Annalise? She needs to eat, too."

"You're Sadie, aren't you?"

"I'm Sadie Louise Brubaker. What's your name besides Jacob?" she asked, her blue eyes big and wide.

"Jacob Joseph Noble. Now, Sadie, go back and sit and don't get up again unless I tell you that you can get up. Understand?"

Sadie nodded vigorously and quickly returned to her place. Annalise wrapped her arm around Sadie, shocked by the little girl's actions.

Jacob turned to the man standing next to him. "Mick, get something for Sadie from the food closet."

"And the others, too," Sadie said. "All of us need something to eat, not just me. I'm not going to eat if everyone doesn't get to eat."

Jacob looked at her for a long moment. "Okay, Sadie, since we want to keep you happy, then Mick will get everyone something to eat."

By that time Tanya and Emily had awakened from their naps. The man named Mick left and returned a few minutes later. He had carrot sticks and apples for all of them. It was hardly a real meal, but at least it was something.

Would they all still be in here when the food closet ran out of snacks? How many men were eating those snacks beside these girls? Were Belinda and Amanda getting something to eat?

She'd hated leaving Amanda there instead of bringing her over here with the rest of the girls, but

she'd been afraid of Jacob's wrath if he knew she'd
gone to the other classroom.

"Do you have lots of friends here with you, Mr.
Jacob?" Sadie asked.

"I got enough, and you talk too much," Jacob
replied.

Annalise pulled Sadie tighter against her side.
"You need not to bother Mr. Jacob anymore," Annalise said to her.

"Maybe if we're all really nice to him, then he
won't kill us," Sadie replied. The matter-of-fact way
the child said it made Annalise wonder how many
times in the past Sadie had thought she'd be killed
by the monster mother who beat her regularly.

Annalise hugged her close. "Honey, I think the
best way to be nice to Mr. Jacob is if we don't talk
to him unless he talks to us first."

"You think about what your teacher just told
you," Jacob said gruffly.

"People in the school." Evan's deep voice sounded
from outside. "We would be glad to work with you
all to get the deceased removed from the premises.
Just let me know how we can get that done."

Annalise tensed as Gretchen came into the room.
"Hey, baby, you need to arrange for them to get the
bodies out of here."

Jacob frowned. "Yeah, yeah."

"Be careful in making the arrangements. Those
cops out there will kill any of us if they get half a
chance."

"I know they'd like to put a bullet in my head."

She smiled at him. "We definitely don't want that. Figure out a plan that gets the dead out and still keeps us all safe." Gretchen placed a hand on his big shoulder. "Figure it out, baby. Take the trash out for me."

Annalise gasped at the woman's callous statements. Dear heaven, what had happened in these people's lives that had made them all so broken?

"Get those bodies into the school lobby as close to the main door as possible," Jacob said. "Then I want everyone in the lobby with their guns ready. If the men who come in to get those bodies try anything, we shoot them on the spot. Tell everyone to be ready and to be in position in fifteen minutes."

"Got it," Gretchen replied, and then left the room.

"Agent Duran," Jacob yelled through the broken window. "In fifteen minutes I'll allow you and two of your men to come to the front door and get the dead. I need to see that you're all unarmed. If I see a gun, we'll shoot. You start walking toward the building on my command. Got it?"

"Can we bring hospital gurneys with us?" Evan asked.

"As long as they are completely bare. I want them stripped down to the metal so there's no place to hide a gun. I'll let you know when it's time to walk." Jacob got up and left the room.

Fifteen minutes. Somehow, someway Annalise needed to make sure Belinda got out with the dead. Otherwise she feared Belinda would become one of the dead, and this might be the only opportunity she got.

"No matter what happens, you girls stay here," Annalise instructed. She had no idea what repercussions there might be for her trying to help Belinda. For all she knew she could be killed. No matter what happened, she needed to know the girls would stay in place whatever went down.

The minutes ticked by with agonizing slowness. Dusk was beginning to fall, with violet shadows seeping into the room through the window.

"Raise up your pants legs so I can see you don't have any ankle holsters," she finally heard Jacob yell out another window. Annalise got up and looked down the hallway that led to the door. Although there were several men standing there, they all had their backs to her, their attention obviously riveted to the front door in the lobby.

It was about to happen. Within minutes FBI agents would be at the front door, and it might be the only way to get Belinda out of here.

She ran across the hallway. "Belinda, you have to get up."

"I can't, Annalise." Tears fell down her cheeks. "I'm too weak and I'm in too much pain."

"You have to try. Amanda, go across the hall and sit with the other girls. You've been very brave so far, and you have to keep being brave."

Amanda got up, tears racing down her cheeks. "Is Miss Belinda going to be okay?"

"I'm going to try to help her. Now go on, honey. Go across the hall," Annalise replied.

Once Amanda was gone, Annalise reached down to Belinda. "Come on, we've got to get you up and on your feet." With Annalise's help, Belinda managed to get to her feet, although she remained crouched forward with her hands over her wound.

"What are we doing? Where are we going?" Belinda asked, and then released a deep moan.

"We're going to try to get you out of here," Annalise said.

She heard Jacob instruct the men outside to start walking toward the building. "Lean on me," she said to Belinda. "I'll help you. We need to get to the front door."

"I can't," Belinda replied.

"You have to. Now, lean on me and let's go." The woman felt fevered, making Annalise even more concerned for her.

Belinda leaned heavily on Annalise as they made their way out of the room and into the hallway. Belinda gasped as she saw the armed men with their backs to them. She stopped walking, her eyes widened with fear.

"Come on, Belinda. This is your only chance." She urged her forward once again. Annalise's heart raced. She had no idea what was going to happen when Jacob saw them. Would he order them both shot?

It didn't matter. They had to take this chance; it might be the only one they had to get Belinda the medical assistance she needed. "Just try to be quiet," Annalise whispered.

The timing had to be perfect. The FBI agents had to be in the school lobby when Annalise shoved Belinda toward them. She stopped walking and listened to Jacob, who was yelling at the agents.

"The bodies are right inside. If you make a move to do anything but get them, then we'll shoot you," he said. "Come in slowly."

With those words, a wave of adrenaline shot through Annalise. She grabbed Belinda firmly by the arm and surged forward. She was half blinded with her need to get Belinda out of the school.

"Hey, what's going on!" one of the men exclaimed as Annalise shoved past him and into the lobby.

She got a brief glimpse of Evan, who held her gaze for only a moment, and two other men with him. She shoved Belinda toward them. "Take her, she needs medical help," she yelled.

A relieved sigh escaped her as Evan took Belinda's arm and pulled her out of the school lobby. At the same time, somebody grabbed Annalise by her hair and yanked her backward.

Pain ripped through her scalp and then shot through her back as she fell to the floor. Gretchen stood over her. She drew back a booted foot and then kicked her in the ribs. Once…twice…three times. The breath whooshed out of Annalise even as she struggled to get to her feet. She glanced back and saw no sign of Belinda.

Despite the pain that racked her, a sweet feeling of success rushed through her. At least Belinda would get the medical treatment she needed and hopefully it would save her life.

Gretchen grabbed her up by the arm and slammed her into the wall. She placed the barrel of her gun under Annalise's chin. Annalise didn't move. She scarcely breathed.

"I should pull this trigger right now," Gretchen said. Her eyes flamed with rage.

"Gretchen," Jacob yelled from the lobby. "Take her back to the classroom. I'll deal with her later."

The woman held the gun on Annalise for another long moment, then lowered it and once again jerked Annalise by the arm. She propelled her down the hallway and shoved her into the classroom.

"Sit down, bitch, and don't move from the wall," Gretchen said.

Annalise slid down the wall next to the girls, who were all crying. "It's okay," she said to them as Gretchen left the room. "We're all okay."

She closed her eyes. Her scalp hurt where her hair had been pulled, and her body ached from the kick she'd received. She didn't know what was going to happen when Jacob came back, but no matter what she knew she'd done the right thing in getting Belinda out so she could receive medical help.

For now, all she could do was gather her strength and wait for the full consequences of her actions. She just hoped she would continue to be here for the sake of the four girls until they were freed from this hell.

Rowan Cooper had dealt with a lot of egotistical, bullheaded small-town cops in her career. She'd also had to try to get along with FBI agents who could be arrogant and rigid and difficult to work with.

Evan was an agent that she not only respected, but also liked to work with. He didn't have an egotistical bone in his body, and he never made any unnecessary drama. The only negative thing she could say about Evan was his tendency for being a bit of a control freak.

He often wasn't great at delegating tasks to his fellow agents and sometimes advice fell on deaf ears, but she certainly couldn't argue with his success rate.

She didn't know how this particular trait might affect his personal life, but when he was in the field working a scene, it was generally an asset.

On this particular case, the problem wasn't Evan, but rather Police Chief Walter Cummings. He was definitely having issues when it came to relinquishing control of the situation to Evan and the other TCD agents.

She'd breathed a little easier when earlier in the day Chief Cummings had left the scene to go home and freshen up. He'd returned just in time to see Evan, Agent Rogers and Agent Brennen getting the dead and one wounded woman out of the school building. Belinda Baker had been rushed to the hospital, and sadly, the bodies of the security guard, the school principal and one other teacher had gone to the morgue.

Since she'd arrived, Rowan had set up hotel rooms for the agents and had spoken to someone from a local café about catering meals to the scene.

She had worked with Evan long enough that she knew he wouldn't take a break until this situation was resolved with the hostages free. He'd remain single-minded and focused no matter how many hours, no matter how many days passed. Then when this was all over, he would go to his hotel room and crash before returning to headquarters in Knoxville.

Her job was to do whatever was in her power to make sure the agents on the scene were well taken care of and left without any outside stress. That meant dealing with the locals. Her biggest job right now was to make sure Chief Cummings didn't do anything to interfere in the operation or undermine Evan.

She now ducked down and carried a sandwich and a bag of chips from the catering truck to where Evan sat in the passenger side of a patrol car. "Evan, you haven't had anything to eat all day long."

"I'm really not hungry," he replied.

"But you know you need to eat," she chided him softly.

He took the food from her. "Thanks, Mom," he replied. His teasing smile lasted only a moment before it was gone and he once again focused on the school building.

Complete darkness had fallen, but the entire area was lit up like daytime thanks to dozens of powerful floodlights. The school was dark except for the occasional glow of a flashlight inside.

"This one is tough, Ro," he said softly. "We're this far into it, and I still don't know what they want. At least if they were making demands I'd have something to work with."

"Thankfully, you managed to get the injured teacher out of there, along with the deceased," Rowan said.

Evan frowned and was silent for a long minute.

"You'll get this right, Evan. You always do," she said with confidence. "Let me know if you need anything else, and I'll see you later."

She remained ducked down and moved away from the scene. She mentally groaned as she spied Chief Cummings beelining for Evan. *What now*, she wondered.

"Chief Cummings," she shouted, hoping to intercept the man before he got to Evan. She ran over to him.

He held up a hand as if to ward her off. "I've got important information to give to Agent Duran."

Rowan bristled at his dismissive gesture but kept her cool. "What kind of information?"

"A 911 call that came in earlier." He held a piece of paper clutched tight against his chest, and in his other hand he held something wrapped in foil. "I have the transcript of the call right here, and it's something Agent Duran needs to see right away."

Rowan followed behind the chief, hoping that whatever he had in his hand was worth bothering

Evan. "Agent Duran, Chief Cummings has some information for you," she said.

Evan frowned at the lawman. "What is it?"

Chief Cumming's chest puffed up with obvious self-importance. "Earlier in the day 911 received a call from a hostage inside the school. She said she and three students are in room 106, and the group who are holding them are called the Brotherhood of Jacob. The call was made by Annalise Taylor and she gave us her number. She said her ringer and notifications are turned off."

Evan took the paper from Chief Cummings and frowned. "Why are we just now getting this information? This call came in much earlier."

"To be honest, I don't know what the holdup was in getting this to us. I'm investigating that now," Chief Cummings replied. "Oh, and this is for you." He held out the aluminum-foil-wrapped item. "A little peace offering. My wife is a hell of a baker. She always says that talent was what kept her from being beaten when she was in foster care. Anyway, it's cranberry and orange bread and she loves giving her baked goods to people I work with."

Rowan held her breath, waiting to see if Evan was going to lose his temper. Thankfully, he murmured a thank-you to the chief, took the bread and then he headed for the mobile van which had arrived early that morning from a nearby FBI office. The van was equipped with all the communication equipment necessary to stay in touch with Hendrick and anyone else they might need to bring this to an end. Rowan was even more grateful that the chief didn't follow Evan, but instead headed back to his squad car.

Chapter Three

Evan had managed to keep his emotions in check and off the fact that Annalise, the woman he had once been deeply in love with, was one of the hostages.

When they had gone in to get the deceased and she'd suddenly appeared, pushing the injured Belinda Baker into their arms, he'd wanted to reach in and grab her out of there, as well.

Then she'd been yanked backward by her hair and out of sight, and Evan had fought against a blinding rage and fear for her. He'd been surprised by the bravery she'd shown to get a fellow teacher help, but he could only hope she was okay now.

In that instant of seeing her again, with her long blond hair loose around her face and her piercing green eyes holding a desperate appeal, he'd wanted to scream to her to run to the safety of his arms.

Annalise had been the second most devastating loss in his life. The first one had forever changed who he was at his core. Losing Annalise, though, had left deep scars on his heart, scars that even after all this time had yet to completely heal.

His mind snapped into sharper focus. He couldn't think about the past right now. He had a job to do that would need his careful attention if the hostages had any hope of walking out unharmed from the horrible situation they were in.

The Brotherhood of Jacob...the name rang a vague bell in his head, but he couldn't access why. At least he finally might gain some information to help him negotiate a way out for those inside.

He hurried to the mobile van, and once inside he tapped on the keys of one of the computers and Hendrick appeared on the screen.

"Evan, talk to me, man," Hendrick said.

"I need you to drop all the other searches you're doing right now and find out everything you can on the Brotherhood of Jacob," Evan replied.

"On it," Hendrick replied, and Evan could hear the immediate clacking of computer keys. He left the van, knowing Hendrick would text him to let him know when he had the information to share.

When they'd gone in to get the deceased, he'd tried to gather as much information as he could. He'd counted six men—maybe seven—and one woman in the lobby, more than enough to guard the two doors in the building. Each one had been armed with either long guns or pistols. They definitely had plenty of firepower.

He returned to his position next to the patrol car and pulled out his phone. At least with Annalise's number, they now had a way to communicate with somebody on the inside. He punched in the number Annalise had given to the authorities and then texted.

Annalise this is Evan. I know you can't answer your phone. Whatever information you can get out to us will be helpful. Let us know you are all ok. We have a whole team working to get you all out safely.

He hesitated a moment and then added, Remember the moon.

He hit the send button and then cursed himself. Why had he felt the need to add that last line? He told himself it was because he wanted her to think of something happy, if only for a moment, while being held hostage.

He believed she had been happy on the night they had shared a midnight picnic in his backyard beneath a full moon. He frowned as another image filled his head and he remembered that moment when she'd been pulled by her hair out of the school lobby.

Was she okay? Had she been badly beaten or worse? Before he could continue with these dark thoughts, he picked up the bullhorn. "People in the school…will you tell me why you're here and what you want so we can bring this situation to a successful end for all of us?"

"People are trying to sleep. I don't want to hear you yapping all night long," the familiar deep voice yelled out the window. "We had to listen to the damned phone ringing all last night. I don't want to hear anything tonight."

"If you walk out of there right now, we can offer you comfortable beds for the remainder of the night," Evan replied. Of course those beds would be in a jail cell.

"Nobody is walking out."

"Can you tell me what you want? I'd really like to work with you," Evan said.

"If you want to work with me, then leave the area. Get all the police out of here."

"You know I can't do that," Evan replied. "Maybe if you release a hostage or two—or at least the children—we could see about moving some people back."

"I'm done talking to you for the night." Gunfire punctuated the words.

Evan cursed. The man was so unpredictable and so uncooperative. He turned and smiled grimly at Daniel as the FBI sniper approached him.

"I've got a spot behind that tree over there where I have a perfect visual of the window where the boss man is located. But he's been very good at staying out of the line of fire," Daniel said. "He's obviously savvy enough to expect a sniper."

"Right now I'm not ready for you to deliver a kill shot," Evan replied. "I'm still hoping I can negotiate everyone out of there. I now have some information that might move things forward."

"I just wanted to let you know I'm set up and ready. Sooner or later he'll make a mistake and I'll get my shot. All I need from you is the go-ahead."

Evan clapped Daniel on the back. "Right now I'm waiting to get more information about this group. I'll let you know if and when I'm ready for you to act."

When Daniel left, Nick walked over to Evan. "Maybe we should go over the blueprints of the school that Hendrick sent us again. Maybe we missed something…some way for us to get inside and get the hostages out."

Evan frowned. "I've already looked at them half a dozen times. They're pretty simple…one door in the front and one door in the back, which makes it pretty easy for just a couple of men to guard from the inside. There's no basement, and right now there is no way to get close enough to the building to get any of our men on the roof. I am thinking that maybe under the cover of night, I might try to get to the van parked by the back door and move it away from the school."

"That would take away any form of transportation they have out of here, although they'd be stupid to attempt to drive it away with the heavy police presence surrounding the area."

"Yeah, but desperate people do desperate things," Evan replied. His phone buzzed with an incoming text message and he read it. "I've got to go," he said to Nick and then hurried toward the mobile van. Hendrick had information.

HENDRICK LEANED FORWARD in his chair, his hand going to a squishy plastic ball he sometimes used for stress relief. And discovering what he had about the Brotherhood of Jacob had sent his stress level through the ceiling.

He now looked at Evan on his computer screen. "The Brotherhood of Jacob was founded eight years ago by a man named Jacob Noble."

"What kind of organization are they?"

Hendrick frowned at his fellow agent. "It has all the markings of a cult masquerading as some sort of church and charity." Old memories slashed through Hendrick's mind, memories of pain, of endless hunger and never-ending fear.

He shook his head to dispel them and released his grip on the squishy ball. Right now more than anything he needed to stay focused and get as much information to Evan as possible.

"They have a membership of about thirty men, fifteen women and ten children. They all live on an off-the-grid compound in the mountains just outside of Pearson. Several of the men have been arrested for a variety of crimes that include bank robbery, stolen firearms, domestic terrorism and murder. But Jacob Noble has no criminal record to date."

Hendrick drew a deep breath and then continued. "Their mission statement is to end world hunger and return power to the righteous."

"And let me guess…this Jacob gets to pick who is righteous," Evan replied dryly. "What can you tell me about Jacob Noble's background?"

"Not much," Hendrick replied. "He was born to poor and modest parents on a farm outside of Raleigh. He married Gretchen Owens three years ago, and I haven't been able to find out much about her. Most of the information I've gained is from Jacob speaking in his official capacity as leader of the group. It looks like they recruit new members by taking to the streets to reach out to people."

"Do you have any more names of the members for me?"

"Only a couple." He told Evan the few names he'd been able to dig up. "For the most part, there seems to be a lot of secrecy surrounding the members, the group and the compound itself. I'm just now starting to dig into the financials to see what might be there, and I'll continue to try to dig into Jacob's background. If I find any other information that will help, I'll be back in touch."

"Thanks, Hendrick."

"Evan, if this man is truly the leader of a cult, then he's a complete narcissist. He'll have made many wonderful promises to the members, and he's probably very charismatic."

"He's definitely not showing much of that particular personality trait right now," Evan replied dryly.

"He's probably angry that he's not in control right now and he's only going to get angrier. Evan, whatever it takes…get those children out of there," Hendrick said fervently.

"I'm working on it. This info will hopefully help." With a murmured goodbye, Evan disappeared from view.

Hendrick continued to stare at the screen as the memories he'd fought off earlier washed over him again. He had been born into a cult and for the first ten years of his life had lived in a compound just outside of Little Rock, Arkansas.

His first memory was of the hunger. The rules of the cult were that the men ate first, women second and then the children were fed whatever was left. And there was never enough food.

There had also been very little love. Children lived separately from their parents, the boys in one house and the girls in another. While his father had occasionally sneaked hugs to Hendrick, his mother had followed the strict guidelines set by the leader, Father Timothy, of no personal interaction.

Hendrick would see his mother out working in the gardens, and as a young boy he'd yearn for her. He wanted her to wrap her arms around him and tell him he was loved. He desperately wanted her to smile at him with love in her eyes, but she remained distant and true to the discipline of the cult.

There were rules for every minute of every day. You woke, you worshipped and you worked long hours. There was not supposed to be any idle chatting among the members, and a punishment always involved physical and emotional pain. Rules changed on a whim, and often even the adults were disciplined for breaking the rules. It was a terrifying way to live.

He was also shocked when he was eight to learn that he had a six-year-old little sister named Elizabeth. He'd immediately gotten close to her. They would whisper together whenever they found themselves working side by side. He tried to protect her from the harsh existence that was everyday life. He sneaked her extra food and hugs. He'd loved her, and he'd believed she loved him back.

She'd been so sweet and in trying to protect and take care of her, Hendrick had taken many beatings. It was after a particularly vicious beating when he'd been ten that his father had come to him in the middle of the night with a plan to escape.

Even though Father Timothy assured them all that the armed guards surrounding the compound were to keep people out, in truth they were there to keep people inside. But Hendrick's father had found a weakness in the security, and that night he intended to exploit it to get his family out.

However, Hendrick's mother and sister had refused to leave. They had chosen the cult over their family. His mother had chosen the cult over him. Hendrick still had plenty of emotional baggage where his mother's total abandonment was concerned.

He sucked in a deep breath, realizing he'd been holding it as his dark memories had raced through his mind. He swiped his hands down the sides of his face, shocked by the light sheen of sweat there.

Remembering his childhood always unsettled him. He was twenty-six-years old, and he'd spent much of the past sixteen years not allowing anyone to dictate much of anything about his life. He'd had enough rigid rules and pain in his first ten years of life.

It had taken a long time for his father and him to

figure out how to live out in the real world. It had also taken a long time for Hendrick to forgive his father for being in the abusive cult and the two to develop a good relationship.

If the Brotherhood of Jacob was anything like the cult he had endured, then he knew the lives of the hostages weren't worth anything. They could easily be sacrificed on the altar of the madness that drove the people who held them.

EVAN STOOD IN the wooded area in the back of the school where dozens of local police officers were stationed. He stared at the black van parked by the back door. Even though Davis and Nick had both volunteered to attempt to move it, Evan knew it was dangerous, and he wasn't going to let anyone do it but himself.

The lights surrounding the building suddenly went dark, just as Evan had arranged. However, he didn't intend to make a move for at least another hour or two.

He was making a calculated guess that nothing would happen with the group in the school during the unexpected lights out. He was hoping they were all tired and hungry and not as alert as they had been earlier in the day.

Moving the van away from the building wasn't an absolute necessity, but with it taken out of the equation it would be one less thing for him to worry about.

From his left he could hear a couple of the police officers talking softly. The clicking and whirring of night insects surrounded him, and a rustle in the brush behind him indicated the presence of a rabbit or other small animal.

Thankfully the moon overhead was mostly hidden by cloud cover, and he'd exchanged his white shirt for a black pullover that Rowan had obtained for him. Even in the dark, Evan could hot-wire a vehicle within minutes.

As he waited for the darkness to deepen, he once again thought about Annalise. It had been almost three years since she'd left him. A job offer took her to a different state, and while he wanted to make the long-distance relationship work, she didn't. He hadn't expected to ever see her again. He certainly hadn't expected to see her being dragged by her long beautiful hair by hostage takers in a school under siege.

The last thing he needed was to let his emotions get hold of him. One of his strengths had always been his complete control over his emotions.

He once again focused on the task at hand. He'd been afraid to raise the bullhorn again after he'd been warned not to, but first thing in the morning he would begin a new approach in an effort to get this situation to a satisfying end. The conversations would be different now that Evan had a little knowledge about the group. Hopefully he would be able to connect better with Jacob Noble and the members of his group.

It was about 2:00 a.m. when he decided to make

his move on the van. He used his radio to alert everyone that he was going in, and then drew a slow deep breath that turned him into a machine with a job to do.

He crouched and raced as fast as he could toward a tree that was halfway between the police line at the edge of a wooded area and the van. When he reached it, he slammed his body to the ground and waited and watched.

He saw no movement from the back of the school where there were six broken-out windows. Maybe nobody was manning this back side of the building during the night.

There was no cover between the tree and the van. Once he left the safety of the tree trunk, he would be completely exposed and vulnerable. He drew another deep breath, resumed a low crouch and then slowly moved toward the van.

He hadn't gone far when shots rang out. Bullets whizzed by him, and once again he hit the ground. More shots came from the school building, and the police presence behind him returned fire in an attempt to provide him cover.

Hoping he wouldn't be shot by the hostage takers or friendly fire, he slithered like a snake back behind the police line at the edge of the woods where Davis waited for him.

The broad-shouldered African American frowned at him. "You shouldn't have taken on that job yourself, man," he said. "I know you like to control your scene, but if you get hurt, those hostages are screwed.

We don't have another hostage negotiator just hanging around."

"Right now I'm just frustrated that it was an epic fail," Evan replied with frustration. "They're more alert in there than I thought they would be after all this time."

"Maybe you should see about getting some sleep while you have a chance," Davis said.

"Yeah, you're probably right." Minutes later the lights were back shining on the building, and Evan was back in the passenger seat of the patrol car. He leaned his head back and closed his eyes, fighting off not only weariness, but also a deep frustration.

When they had arrived here earlier in the day, he'd hoped to get the hostages out by nightfall. He was disturbed that hadn't happened.

He could only hope that when morning came Jacob would be more agreeable to having a conversation that would see the safe release of the hostages.

If that didn't happen, Evan would need to consider other, more dangerous options. That thought kept him awake for a very long time.

Chapter Four

The gunfire coming from the back of the building jolted Annalise. Thankfully the noise hadn't awakened the girls, who were likely too emotionally and physically exhausted.

She raised her hand and touched her swollen lower lip. When Jacob had come back in the room after she'd gotten Belinda to safety, he'd backhanded her hard enough to rattle her brain. She'd just been grateful that he hadn't killed her.

She had a feeling the only reason that she was still alive was to deal with the girls and keep them as quiet as possible.

Once the gunfire began, Jacob cursed and ran out of the room, and Annalise took the opportunity to run to her phone and snatch it off the charger. She returned to her place against the wall, her heart banging unsteadily as she held the phone tightly in her hand.

When the gunfire stopped, Jacob didn't return and she could hear him yelling in a room down the hallway. She pulled her phone up so the screen was visible.

She had one message. She opened it and read the note from Evan. Thank goodness the 911 call she'd made had gotten through to him. It gave her some solace knowing that of all the people in the world, her life and the lives of the girls were in his hands. She knew just how good he was at what he did, how utterly devoted he was to the job.

Remember the moon.

Tears blurred her vision as she read those words. They were tears of exhaustion and the sweet memory of tremendous love. *Remember the moon*. She wondered why he had texted that to her. Even as she thought about it, she realized the answer was probably that he wanted her to have a happy thought to help her through this horrible ordeal.

And the memory of that night under a full moon in his backyard was more than just a happy place in her heart, it was a place of warmth and love with the man who, at that time, she'd believed would be her partner through life.

She looked toward the doorway, wondering how much time she had before Jacob came back into the room. Maybe he wouldn't return for the rest of the night. She'd seen a weight of exhaustion riding his big shoulders. She suspected there weren't enough men with him to rotate the guard duty at all the doors and windows and also get enough sleep. Maybe this was the night the leader of this group would find someplace in the building to hole up and sleep until morning.

The phone burned in her hand. Her need to reach out to Evan and hear his voice was nearly over-whelming, but so was her fear of somehow getting caught.

Jacob was already angry with her about Belinda. If he caught her with the phone talking to the out-side authorities, she wasn't convinced that Jacob wouldn't kill her, or get his wife to do the dirty work. If that happened, then who would be here to protect the girls? Who would soothe them when they cried?

She began to softly hum, her gaze going once again to the doorway. She looked back at the phone and Evan's message, and her fingers hit the phone icon.

He answered before the first ring had completely finished. "Annalise."

She squeezed her eyes tightly shut at the sound of his familiar deep voice. "Evan," she whispered into the phone, and once again kept her gaze on the doorway.

"Are you all right? Are you safe to talk?" His voice held the same kind of urgency that sizzled through her body.

"I'm okay…and I'm safe for now. There are four students with me and we're all okay. We're hungry and tired and just want to get out of here." Tears blurred her vision. "Is Belinda okay? Have you heard anything about her condition?"

"I'm sorry, I haven't, but I know she's in the hospital where she belongs."

"They didn't even want to release her, but I was afraid if I didn't get her out of here, she would have died."

"I saw somebody grab you by your hair…were you hurt?"

"No, I'm okay," she said, and then ran her tongue over her swollen lip. "Jacob is crazy, but his wife, Gretchen, is pure evil."

"Annalise, do you know what these people want? Have you heard a reason why they burst into the school in the first place?"

"I don't know what they want. I've asked and asked, but I don't know what they want or why they're here," she replied helplessly. She wished she had the answers so Evan would have the information he needed to do his job.

"I'm using every resource I have to get you all out of there safely," he said. "You just need to be patient and stay safe."

"I know. I just want these girls out of here. If you can get them to release any hostages, it's got to be the girls who get out."

"I want you all out safely," he replied. He asked her several more logistical questions. Then, "I couldn't believe it when I heard you were in there. I thought you were teaching at a college in Missouri."

"I was, but I got this offer to work here and I needed a change. These kids…oh Evan, they are wonderful. They are so bright and so loving."

"Uh… I have to ask this next question… Do you have a spouse we need to contact for you?"

"No significant other." She looked toward the doorway to assure that she was still safe to talk. There were so many questions she wanted to ask him. They were personal questions that had no place in what was happening right now.

"Evan, are we going to get out of here?"

"We'll do whatever it takes to make that happen." She could hear the determination in his voice.

She pressed the phone more closely to her ear and made sure the girls were sleeping. "Evan, I'm scared." The words fell from her lips before she'd fully realized they were in her head. "I'm trying to act so brave for the children, but inside I'm just as terrified as they are."

"Annalise, I want you to stay afraid. It might be that fear that keeps you on your toes and alive," he said.

"I always hated it when you were blunt with me," she replied with a panic-stricken laugh. A short, awkward moment of silence ensured.

In that moment flashes of the times they'd shared together swept through her mind. He'd always made her feel like a sexy, passionate woman whenever he'd gazed at her with a hunger in his dark brown eyes.

Their backgrounds couldn't have been more different. He had grown up poor and on the streets of the Bronx while she came from wealthy, nurturing parents in Knoxville. A chance meeting in a coffee shop in Knoxville had been the beginning of a two-year relationship that had ended with her making the difficult, but necessary decision to leave him, and ultimately she'd taken the job offer in Missouri to make the break a clean one.

"Are you still there?" His voice broke through the memories.

"For now, but if Jacob comes back I'll need to disconnect quickly. He has no idea I have the phone, and he's got a nasty temper. His wife's is even worse."

"For God's sake, Annalise, don't take any unnecessary chances."

"I know it's been a long time, but maybe you could give me a big hug when I get out of here?" Tears once again burned at her eyes. "I'm sorry, I sound so pathetic."

"You don't. You just need to stay strong until that can happen."

"I'm working on it."

"Can you tell me if there are any weaknesses in the guards, anyplace or anything we can exploit to get you all out of there?"

"I know they didn't plan for this. They wanted to get in and out for whatever reason before any police arrived. They're eating snacks we keep in here for the students, but that isn't going to last long. I also think there's some in-fighting among the group."

"That's all helpful to know. Anything else?"

She frowned thoughtfully. "I can't think of anything."

"That's okay. You're doing a great job," he said encouragingly.

She leaned her head back against the wall. "Evan… I'm sorry about how things ended between us."

"I have a lot of regrets, too," he replied softly. "I…"

She heard footsteps approaching from the hall and hit the disconnect button on the phone. She slid it under her thigh just before Jacob walked into the room.

He turned and stared at her with narrowed eyes. Although there were no lights on in the classroom, he was visible from the bright lights shining in from the outside. "I thought I heard talking in here."

Her heart banged against her ribs beneath his suspicious glare. "I was humming to myself. It's how I self-soothe in a stressful situation."

Dear God, she hoped he bought it. If he didn't, and for some reason he made her stand up, then he would find the phone. She held eye contact with him as her heart continued to race and finally he grunted. "Don't do it again," he warned, and then headed to his chair near the window.

She released a shuddery sigh of relief and felt the burn of the phone beneath her leg. It was her lifeline to the outside…to Evan.

Once again she leaned her head back and closed her eyes. Images of Evan chased through her mind, images of happy times they had spent together.

She'd known the very first time she'd seen him that he was going to be somebody special in her life. It had been a Saturday morning, and she'd been getting a coffee in her favorite café. The shop was crowded, but she'd managed to claim one of the small, round tables near the front window.

The minute she'd seen him walk in, her heart had jolted. She couldn't help but notice how good-looking he was. When he'd approached her and asked to share her table, she'd readily agreed. That day they had spent two hours talking together.

She finally drifted off to sleep and dreamed of the midnight picnic under the full moon. He'd surprised her that night. He'd picked her up at her apartment at dusk and then had taken her to his backyard, where he had a blanket spread out on the close-cropped lawn. He'd had chicken salad sandwiches and fresh strawberries, chunks of her favorite cheese and champagne.

In her dream she was in his big, strong arms and he was kissing her with all the passion of a man in love. She'd believed he loved her as she did him. She had believed on that night they would eventually get married.

She awoke suddenly, unsure what had roused her. Darkness still filled the room and she heard the heavy, deep breathing of Jacob. She released a deep sigh. Not only had love not been enough to keep her and Evan together, but now she had to face the real possibility that she'd have no future…the possibility that she wouldn't get out of here alive.

HEARING ANNALISE'S VOICE filled with such fear had shot arrows of pain through Evan. Hearing her voice had also renewed the deep ache he'd felt when she had left him. It had taken him a very long time to get over her. If he was honest with himself, there were days and nights he still didn't think he was quite over her.

But he couldn't focus on the past. Still, for the past nearly three years he'd been haunted by the what-ifs. Regrets? Hell yes he had regrets. He spent the rest of the night thinking about those regrets as he also processed the information she'd given him...information that might help bring this situation to an end.

It was good that there was a limited food source, and it was definitely good if the hostage takers were fighting among themselves.

While he waited for the darkness of night to pass, he gathered his thoughts for the emotional assault he intended to launch at daybreak.

He could have used the bullhorn and bellowed at them all night long, but he hadn't trusted Jacob not to lose it completely. He'd threatened to toss out dead little girls when a phone had rung all night. Evan didn't want to give him a reason to go off about being shouted at all night long.

Meanwhile, Chief Cummings was badgering him for an all-out attack on the building, something Evan feared might result in the injury or death of the hostages if not also official personnel. He finally had a name and some information about the group to use, and he also believed the hunger issue might bring this all to an end before force needed to be used.

Was his hesitancy with the option of using force to go in because he knew Annalise was inside? Was he allowing that fact to influence the decisions he needed to make? No, it didn't matter who was in that building; force was always the very last option used in any hostage case.

Evan could be very patient. He knew that was one of his strengths as a negotiator. He'd rather get this done right than get it done fast. Chief Cummings was just going to have to live with the decisions made. If he tried to do anything behind Evan's back, Evan would see the man brought up on charges.

He hoped Annalise would get an opportunity to speak to him again, but the rest of the night passed without any more contact. As always, one of his fears was that she had or would get caught with the phone.

The standoff had begun on a Tuesday with the locals, and within hours it was going to be Thursday morning. That meant the armed men had been in the building for two nights and days with only snack food to eat. Surely that food was running out. It wouldn't feed grown men for an indefinite amount of time.

Regina Sandhurst had arrived at the scene earlier in the evening. She was a petite brunette whose main residence was in New York, but she also had a condo in Pearson and had assured them that she would remain here until the hostages were free.

She had tried to be as helpful as possible, but she had no clue what the people in the school might be after. She brought with her a list of all the deliveries that were made on a regular basis to the school, along with a list of everyone on staff. She'd left for her condo at dusk with the promise to be back this morning.

He heard from Hendrick once again with information about some of the financials of the group. So far everything appeared to be aboveboard, but the tech guru was still chasing down a few things. Evan knew if anything was hidden, Hendrick would find it. The man matched Evan in his passion and commitment to his job.

It was just after dawn when he picked up the bullhorn once again. "Jacob Noble and men in the school. I understand the goal of the Brotherhood of Jacob is to end world hunger. That's a wonderful goal to be pursuing."

"Is this the part where you try to be my friend so I'll give up?" Jacob yelled out the window. "Sorry, Agent Duran, I'm not buying what you're selling. I don't want to be your friend."

In another circumstance Evan might have unarmed himself as a show of good faith, and he would attempt to walk to the building for an up close and personal meeting with Jacob.

But the fact that he was so quick to fire his weapon indiscriminately with no provocation at all kept Evan from attempting it. As Davis had reminded him earlier, a dead hostage negotiator certainly wouldn't help matters.

"I want you to scale down and back up the police presence, and I need a bulletproof van for our use," Jacob yelled.

"It would take me some time to arrange something like that," Evan replied. "How about you let all the hostages go, and I'll see what I can do to accommodate you."

"You accommodate me, and then we'll talk about letting the hostages go. This conversation is now over." He fired a burst of bullets out the window.

"Big surprise that he wants a bulletproof van to get out of here," Nick said. He was a good man with a family of his own. Evan had worked with him several times before and admired the man's dedication to his wife and kids and the job.

"Don't they all," Evan replied dryly. "But sooner or later they're going to get hungry. According to Annalise, they've been eating snacks that were there for the students, but they won't last long."

"At least you have some leverage there," Nick replied.

"Yeah, I just hate the idea of those kids being hungry." And Annalise—he couldn't imagine what she was going through. He also couldn't allow his thoughts to dwell on her. He had to keep all his emotions in check to do the best job possible. Thoughts of Annalise and his relationship with her would only be distracting.

As Nick moved away, Evan raised the bullhorn once again. "People in the school, I'm sure you all must be getting hungry. If you want some food brought to you, then all you need to do is release the hostages."

There was a long silence, and then Jacob's gun came out the window. "I'm not releasing any of the hostages, and we're doing just fine in here. All you need to do is move back your men and get me an armored van."

"I told you I'm not working on that for you until the hostages are released," Evan replied.

"You've got this all backward. I'm the one in charge here," Jacob yelled. "Do what I ask, and I'll let the hostages go."

"Maybe some of your men would like some egg sandwiches," Evan replied. "I'm sure that teacher and the four little girls you have in there are getting hungry. Maybe your wife would like a hot breakfast sandwich, too."

This time there was a longer pause. Evan imagined Jacob was wondering just how much information the authorities knew about what was happening inside the school. He probably figured Belinda would have given Evan information about who was inside and that Jacob's wife was one of the hostage takers.

"Jacob, I'd like to understand what your goal is. Could you tell me why you went into the school? How were you looking to advance your goal by forcefully entering the school? If I understand your position better, then maybe we can agree on some things."

"You don't need to understand anything," Jacob replied.

"The offer for food still stands," Evan yelled. "Release the hostages, and a hot breakfast will be delivered to the doorstep."

Suddenly Jacob fired out the window. "Shut up about the food. I'm not interested in anything but you getting me an armored van and promising me and my people safe passage out of here, and that's all I got to say to you."

"We're talking in circles, Jacob. The only way I can even think about doing that is when the hostages have all been released," Evan replied. "Maybe you could release a couple of hostages to show your good faith. After that happens we can talk about how you and your men can get out of the school."

Silence.

The silence wasn't necessarily a bad thing. What he hoped was happening was that some of the men were trying to talk some sense into Jacob. Annalise had suspected some in-fighting, and Evan definitely wanted to exploit that. He was hoping that hunger was what would ultimately drive a wedge between Jacob and his followers.

His phone rang. Annalise was on a video call. He answered it. He'd only had a quick glimpse of her before, but now he was rendered speechless as he drank in the sight of her.

Her blond hair was longer than it had been the last time he'd seen her, but her eyes were just as green. His chest tightened as he saw her red, swollen lower lip.

She wore a pink blouse that looked rumpled, but

he couldn't dwell on how she looked. Instead, he focused on her surroundings.

Behind her was a plain white wall that gave no clue as to exactly where she and the children were in the room. Thankfully she'd already told him they were seated against the south wall in the classroom. The school faced north.

"Evan…" she said softly, and her eyes filled with tears.

"What happened to your lip?" he asked as a small knot of anger tightened his chest.

She shook her head. "It was the price I paid for getting Belinda help. It's no big deal."

It was a very big deal to him. It let him know that Jacob not only had the ability to kill when he thought necessary, but he'd also rough up the hostages as he saw fit. "Are you sure you're safe to talk?"

She nodded. "For now it's okay. They're all in another room, and I can hear them arguing. Some of the men want to give up. They're hungry and afraid."

"That's a good thing," he replied. "How are you and the girls doing?"

"We're all hungry and tired of being here, but we're hanging in."

He could see the deep exhaustion in her eyes, and he ached for her and the children he knew she was comforting to the best of her ability. "I'm doing everything possible on my end."

She smiled. "I know. It gives me great comfort to know that the best hostage negotiator in the world is on the case."

He'd believed he'd moved on from her, from what had been them, but that smile of hers shot a rivulet of unexpected heat through him. God, he wanted her, he wanted all of them out of there.

"I just want you to stay safe until I get you out of there," he said. "Whatever you do, don't get caught with the phone, Annalise. Jacob will get more and more desperate and angry as he continues to lose control of everything."

"We're being smart," she replied. "Sadie has been helping me by acting as a lookout so I can get the phone off and on the charger. Right now I can still hear the men yelling and arguing with each other. I just… I just needed to see your face."

"It's good to see you, too." He swallowed against a rise of emotions and reminded himself that emotions had no place in this environment.

"I like the beard. It looks good on you," she commented.

"Thanks."

Her smile was so soft, he wanted to reach right through the phone and pull her into his arms. But just that quickly her features registered alarm, and her face disappeared and the line disconnected. Damn. His heart thundered loudly in his ears. He hoped she hadn't just got caught.

He drew a deep breath and turned to look at the scene behind him, where news trucks had begun to gather the evening before. This morning more had joined the rigs already parked. It was not only local reporters; national news organizations had also arrived.

Rowan had been busy with the ever-growing crowd, and so far had done a terrific job of using some of the local police to keep the press far away from the immediate scene.

She'd even set up a podium so that throughout the day Chief Cummings could do news updates. Hopefully that would keep him busy and feeling important while Evan did all the hard negotiating behind the scenes and not get any of the credit for the eventual release of the hostages. Not that he cared about credit…he just cared about the ultimate results.

"Nick—" he turned to the man who had just approached "—why don't you get Davis and Daniel and meet me at the mobile van," he said. "I need some updates." He also needed to refocus on the task at hand and not on his past with Annalise.

Within minutes the four men were huddled by the side of the mobile van. "Daniel, tell me what's going on at the compound where these people live." The agent was not only a skilled sniper, he'd also been working with the local police and Hendrick per Evan's instructions.

"According to what Hendrick could find out, there's only one way in and one way out of the place. The entire compound is surrounded by a high fence and guarded, but we now have a heavy presence at the gates. We're checking out any vehicles that go in and come out. If any of these scumbags manage to get out of here, they won't be able to go home to roost."

"Good. Anything to report, Davis?"

Davis frowned. He'd been working with the local police to make sure the back of the building was being guarded, and that men were on call for a potential entry into the school.

"The men are complaining about working so many hours, but I think the gunfire out the back windows when you tried to get to the van woke them up as to just how serious the situation is," he said.

"As if armed men holding five hostages wasn't serious enough?" Evan replied with disgust.

"With all the action happening at the front of the building, I think they forgot that they needed to stay on their toes. Besides, I have a feeling the toughest crime scene those men have seen is in a convenience store where a lollipop was stolen," Davis said with equal disgust.

"Chief Cummings is constantly crowing about how good his men are," Daniel said.

"Let's hope his men are good," Evan said. "We need them to be good. What about the interviews, Nick. How are they coming?"

"We've now interviewed all the teachers who work here, but none of them had any information about what's going on. I know Hendrick is checking into their backgrounds. We're also working off the list Regina Sandhurst gave us of the other staff and delivery services, and will be conducting interviews with them throughout the afternoon. I also spoke to Director Pembrook earlier," Nick continued. "She didn't want to bother you, but she told me to tell you to take your time and don't feel pressured by either the locals or the news reports."

"Hell, you all know me well enough to know I don't give a damn about what any of the reporters say about me," Evan replied. "And Chief Cummings isn't about to push me to do anything I'm not ready to do."

"You know we all trust your judgment," Nick replied. "We're all behind you."

Evan clapped him on the back. "Thanks, man. Let's all check back in with each other in about two hours. I know we're all tired, but stay on your toes. I intend to start really putting on some pressure, and you all know that things can change in the blink of an eye."

Evan returned to his position at the patrol car, his head swirling with thoughts and information. Under different circumstances, he would have seriously considered telling Daniel to get into position and shoot Jacob.

There was really only one reason holding him back from doing that, and that was Annalise's assessment that Jacob's wife was even more evil than her husband. If Jacob was taken out by a sniper's bullet, he worried about what Gretchen might do. So, right now killing Jacob wasn't an option.

This would also usually be the time he'd tell the people inside that he needed proof that the hostages were still alive.

But the last thing he wanted was for Jacob to drag Annalise and the girls up to a window knowing that she was hiding her phone. Besides, he knew the hostages were still alive thanks to Annalise keeping him informed.

He raised the bullhorn. "Brotherhood of Jacob members, if you tell me what you want and why you are in the school, we might be able to work something out. We need to have an open dialogue."

There was no response from Jacob. Evan waited fifteen minutes and then delivered the same message. Again there was no reply.

Evan hoped Jacob's men were becoming mutinous. He hoped like hell that hunger, discomfort and isolation were making the men rebellious against the leader who had put them in this situation in the first place. And for what? What on earth had drawn them to the school building where there was nothing but a closet full of snack food?

The school office had no money. They still hadn't asked for any kind of a ransom. They'd made no contact with Regina Sandhurst, so what in the hell were they doing here? What had been their initial plan?

Damn it, what had they been looking for when they'd barged into the school with guns blazing? It was the one question, despite all the resources at his fingertips, he'd been unable to answer.

He raised the bullhorn to his mouth once again. "Jacob Noble, tell me what you and your men want. Why are you inside the school and what is it you were after? Talk to me about your mission. Help me understand."

There was still no response. This had now become an ominous silence. He had a gut feeling this hostage situation was coming to a head. He also had a bad feeling because he couldn't see exactly how it would end.

HENDRICK HAD A bad feeling. This whole standoff situation at the school was going on for too long, and according to Evan, there had been absolutely no give at all from the hostage takers. The man in charge was not having any real dialogue with Evan.

Unfortunately, Hendrick hadn't been able to figure out what the group had wanted when they'd stormed the school. He'd searched every avenue he had to try to find the answer without any success.

Even though he had 100 percent faith in Evan, Hendrick knew the man had been thrown for a loop when he'd learned Annalise Taylor was one of the hostages.

Hendrick remembered just how crazy Evan had been over her. He'd talked about her all the time while the two had been dating. Hendrick also remembered how utterly devastated his friend had been when Annalise had left Knoxville to go teach at a private college in Missouri.

He couldn't imagine what kind of conflict had to be swirling inside Evan's head knowing that she was one of the hostages in the school. He'd always suspected Evan hadn't really gotten over her.

Even though the minute she'd left town he had stopped talking about her, Hendrick believed Evan had brooded about her far more often than he'd ever admit.

None of your business, he told himself. Still, their love for each other had seemed so strong, so real to Hendrick.

He was definitely a skeptic when it came to love. He was smart enough to know that his mother's abandonment and the lack of love earlier in his life had certainly fed into his beliefs. He rarely dated, preferring time on a computer to putting himself out into the dating scene.

At least his computers never rejected him. The computers understood his quirkiness and his need to sometimes control his environment.

He frowned. The last thing he needed to be thinking about was his own particular list of dysfunctions. He reminded himself that his only job here was to provide support and research that might give Evan more tools in his toolbox.

To that end Hendrick had been digging up anything and everything he could about Jacob Noble and his group of followers. He now leaned back in his chair and scrubbed at his burning, tired eyes with his fists.

He'd managed to chase down all the financials of the Brotherhood of Jacob and everything appeared aboveboard, but in digging into Jacob Noble's personal finances, he was running into some interesting discrepancies.

Jacob Noble and his followers might lead a simple, back to the earth kind of lifestyle on the compound, but Jacob and his wife owned some property in the Caymen Islands, and Hendrick suspected they were also hiding a sizable amount of funds there.

Hendrick was still trying to confirm it. He'd given this information to Evan in their last face-to-face, and he hoped like hell his friend could use it to finally bring this all to an end. Surely Jacob's followers would be interested to hear that their leader wasn't being aboveboard with them and instead was lining his own pockets.

One thing Hendrick knew for sure—if Evan wasn't successful in getting Annalise out of that building alive and well, then Evan would never, ever be the same again.

As THE DAY wore on, Evan was on the bullhorn every fifteen minutes trying to get a dialogue going with Jacob. The only communication happening was the cult leader screaming and cursing and shooting at him.

There was no question Evan was getting frustrated. Jacob was forcing his hand by not being willing to communicate in a meaningful way.

It was as if the man was so far gone in his own head and into his need for control, he didn't recognize that he and his followers were in a lose-lose situation. They had no food and no way out. So, how long would it take for them to finally break? Were they going to break, or was Evan going to have to go in forcefully when and if he had an opportunity that would hopefully not endanger the hostages.

The weather had gotten cooler and the sky overhead had become cloudy and gray, reflecting Evan's current mood. Thankfully Rowan had kept Chief Cummings busy giving regular updates to the press. It was obvious the chief was loving the limelight and his time in front of the cameras. That worked just fine with Evan.

It was late afternoon when he decided to use another tactic. "If any of you men want to just walk out of there, all you have to do is put your weapons down and come out the front door with your hands up over your head."

If what Annalise had told him about the infighting was true, then hopefully he could turn a couple of the men inside and get them to walk out. Eventually, surely that would make Jacob surrender the hostages and come out before anyone else got hurt.

"We will not fire on you if you put your hands up and come out peacefully," he said.

"It would be nice if they'd all just walk out of there," Nick said. "I can't believe that none of the men inside have grown weary of this whole thing."

"If we can get a couple of them to surrender, then I'm hoping Jacob will give up, too," Evan replied. "He's definitely in a delusional state of mind if he thinks he's going to outlast us or that I'm going to provide an armored van and just let them all drive away from this."

"At least if one man walks out maybe he'd be able to give us some information, like how many men are really in there and what in the hell they were after when they forced their way into the school," Nick replied.

Davis appeared at Evan's side. "Just wanted to let you know Regina Sandhurst is back on scene. Right now she's over by the food truck."

"Thanks. I think I'll go check in with her." Evan headed toward the food truck in the distance.

"Agent Duran," Regina greeted him with a grim smile. "Any progress being made?"

"Unfortunately not much. I was wondering if any of the hostage takers have contacted you yet to pay a ransom? We were wondering if that's a possible motive."

"Nobody has contacted me," she replied. "I almost wish somebody had so we'd know that was what they're after."

"It was just a long shot," Evan replied in frustration.

"You know I'll do anything I can to help bring this all to an end," she said. "I just feel so helpless, and I fear this bad publicity is going to affect the donations that keep the school running."

"Hopefully that won't happen," Evan replied. She obviously didn't realize that she sounded a little cold worrying about donations while there were lives on the line.

"You'll keep me updated on any information you get? I want to know absolutely everything that's going on," she replied. "I don't want to get my information from that pompous ass we call a police chief."

"I'll be sure and keep you informed," he replied, although he didn't remark about her assessment of Chief Cummings.

The two spoke for a few more minutes and then Evan returned to his position. The breeze had picked up a bit and tossed around the leaves on the nearby trees.

Under different circumstances the scene before them would have been quite pretty and peaceful. The two blond brick buildings sat on manicured, lush green grass with the tall, mature trees and bushes adding to the attractive landscape.

But there was nothing pretty about the scene as far as Evan was concerned. He saw each tree trunk as a potential place for a shooter from the school to hide behind. The colorful blowing leaves were nothing more than a distraction.

In all his years of hostage negotiation, he'd never had a hostage taker who didn't want to talk about themselves and what they wanted. Most hostage takers couldn't wait to tell the world what was going on in their life and what had brought them to the situation they were in.

Jacob was definitely an anomaly in that he had no apparent desire to talk about himself or what he and his followers were doing. His unwillingness to do so made Evan's training pretty much go out the window in this situation.

He now groaned at the sight of Chief Cummings approaching with Rowan hurrying just behind him. "Agent Duran, a word," the chief said.

"About what?" Evan asked.

"My men are tired, and I'm running out of funds for all the extra personnel we're using. It's past time to end all this."

"We're all tired," Evan replied curtly. "I'm sure you can work something out with the local council concerning the funding for the extra personnel."

"We need to coordinate going in with force and bringing this to an end right now," Chief Cummings continued. "My men are all ready to go."

"We're not going in with force at this point," Evan replied firmly. "I have information that the men inside are now arguing. I don't think it will be long before some of the men walk out of there. We just need to sit tight and wait for that to happen."

"I disagree with you. My men and I are tired of sitting tight." The man took a step closer to Evan. "This should have already been over. We have enough men to take the building by storm, and that's what we need to do. Besides, having all these men here is leaving the streets of my city unsafe."

"You have the right to reassign some of your men to wherever you need them. We've got this situation covered." Evan drew in a deep breath as he felt his patience slipping and his anger with the man rising.

"The community is pressing me to act!" Chief Cummings exclaimed.

"I don't give a damn what anyone says. I don't take advice from a mob."

Chief Cummings's nose flared in obvious frustration. "You don't care about the local attention because once this is all done and over, you all will just pack your bags and leave. My men and I have to still live and work here."

"I'll take the next presser on your behalf," Rowan said, and stepped between the two men. "Chief Cummings, I'll make sure they know how much we appreciate your support and how helpful you and your officers have been."

The chief grunted, but he didn't step back from Evan. "I still think you're making a big mistake not ending this right now."

"Why in the hell would I risk the hostages' lives by going in with force? Have you forgotten that there are four children inside the building? Right now they're alive, and I want to make sure I keep them that way." Evan's anger rose higher as he glared at the man before him. "Eventually fatigue and hunger will drive them out, and we won't need to use force."

Rowan placed her hand on the chief's shoulder. "Come on, Chief, let's go over the progress so far. I'm sure reporters are eager to hear from you again."

God bless Rowan, for if Evan had to continue to face off with the man, he might have wound up punching him in his pugnacious face. Thankfully, as it was, the potential of getting in front of the cameras again and his reputation lifted by Rowan's words of praise appealed to him more than standing his ground with Evan.

"That man is a complete and total joke," Nick said once Rowan and the chief walked away. "He's also a big jerk."

"He's definitely getting on my last nerve," Evan replied. "I'm just not ready to do something drastic right now to bring this to an end. We've only been working this for the last twenty-four hours."

"You're definitely right that holding out is the way to go, especially with the kids in there."

Evan nodded. "I really believe at this point it's just a matter of us outwaiting them."

He stared at the school building. At least for now the hostages were alive. He could only hope they remained that way and he was making the right choice.

Chapter Five

"Mr. Jacob, could we have something else to eat?" Sadie asked.

Jacob was once again in his position in a chair to the side of the window. He turned to look at Sadie. "There's nothing left," he replied. "And I don't want any of you whining or crying that you're hungry. I don't like whiners almost as much as I hate screamers."

Annalise tightened her arm around Sadie. "What does the Brotherhood of Jacob do?" Annalise asked. "Why did you form this group in the first place?" She held her breath, wondering what his response would be to her questions and if somehow she might be able to make sense of what was going on.

"Society has got no place for people like me. I've got no formal education, and I grew up dirt-poor with a mother who screamed at me and beat me half to death every other day of my life."

"I'm sorry you had to endure that," Annalise said.

He frowned. "Everyone today is out for them-selves, and nobody is tending to the poor and hungry. We've got homeless and starving people on the streets of our cities, and nobody is interested in helping them. The Brotherhood of Jacob brought together people who want to help."

"So what does the Brotherhood of Jacob do to help?" Annalise asked. Any information she could glean might help Evan.

"We grow vegetables and take boxes to the homeless on the streets. We also sell them and send money to charities we deem are appropriate." A scowl stretched across his forehead. "Nobody ever gave me a helping hand. Now I've got the power in the Brotherhood of Jacob, and I decide who we help and when."

"So what about your wife? I guess she has the same views you do?"

An unexpected grin lifted his lips. "Gretchen hates almost everyone but me. She grew up in the foster care system where she was abused nearly every single day of her life. She learned young that nobody was on her side. But she's found her place with me and within the arms of the Brotherhood."

"So how does being here in the school help anyone?"

Before he could reply, Gretchen walked in. "Everything okay in here?" she asked with a smile at Jacob.

"Yeah, except the teacher has a lot of questions," he replied.

Gretchen turned and stared at Annalise and then looked back at her husband. "Let me know if you need me to shut her up. I'll be glad to knock her teeth in."

Jacob laughed. "That's my girl…always willing to go the extra mile for her man."

My God, who were these people? Annalise wondered when Gretchen had left the room again. What had life done to them to twist them so badly?

Despite Jacob's brief laughter, there was no question there was a new tension in the man in charge. He'd screamed at his men throughout the day, and even as he now sat silently at the window she could feel a deranged kind of tension radiating from him.

She was concerned for the girls, who were lethargic and sleeping too much of the time. Now, knowing there was no more food for them made her even more worried.

How long could this go on? How long would these men go without food and being exhausted? What was the endgame? Was Jacob crazy enough to commit mass murder and then kill himself? Far too often these kinds of situations ended that way.

No, she had to stop thinking so negatively. She shouldn't go to such dark places in her mind. Surely after all this time, one way or another, these precious girls would be saved. She would do all she could to make sure of it. She had to keep believing that. She absolutely couldn't lose all hope.

Dusk had fallen once again, and Jacob stood and stretched. Annalise's heart beat a little bit faster in anticipation of him leaving the room.

She quickly closed her eyes and pretended to be

asleep. Her heart still thudded rapidly in her chest. The minute she heard his heavy footsteps leaving the room, she sprang into action.

She rushed to her phone, grabbed it and returned to her position. With Jacob still gone, she hit the button that brought up Evan's ruggedly handsome face on the screen. "Evan," she whispered, for a moment overcome with so many emotions she could say nothing more.

"Annalise, are you and the kids still okay?"

She nodded. "We're okay, but the snack food is gone."

"I know it's tough, but that's a good thing. It will make the men more apt to walk out of there. I'm sorry that you and the kids have to do without until that happens."

She nodded again, knowing there was nothing that could be done to change the situation right now. "Talk to me, Evan. I need to have something else in my mind besides fear." She quickly glanced to the doorway and then relaxed as she heard Jacob yelling someplace else in the building.

His smile was soft. "We had a lot of good times together," he said.

"Yes, we did." How she wished she could have those wonderful times again with him. "I've thought about those good times a lot during the past three years."

"Yeah, me, too," he replied.

"I wish—"

"You all stop your bitching and stick with me." Jacob's voice boomed from just outside the doorway.

Annalise hung up and hid the phone beneath her thigh, then closed her eyes and once again pretended to be asleep. She sensed him staring at her for a couple of long moments and then heard his heavy footsteps as he walked across the room. The chair near the window creaked beneath his weight.

As the night wore on, he left the room one more time and she managed to get her phone back on the charger. Finally she fell into an exhausted sleep without dreams.

When she awakened again, it was morning. Once the girls were up, Jacob escorted them to the bathroom. "Listen, girls," Annalise said. "There is no more food for anybody. Drink as much water as you can since that is all you're getting." They drank using their hands as cups.

"Can't we get out of here?" Tanya asked. "I want to be back in my own room."

"Me, too." Emily broke down in tears. "I'm tired of being here. I'm so tired of being scared."

Annalise hugged the little girl close and then released her. "We need to stay strong. You all know by now that Jacob doesn't like crying. I know it's hard, but we've all got to keep our emotions in check until somebody gets us out of here."

It was going to be a difficult day. The girls were fussy, and Annalise did her best to give them a pep talk, not only to keep them strong, but also to keep them alive.

When they returned to the classroom, the girls once again took their positions against the wall, but Annalise remained standing.

"Jacob, I want the girls to sit at the desks and work today," she said.

One of his bushy black eyebrows shot up. "Who made you boss today?" he sputtered with a laugh of disbelief. "I don't give a damn what you want."

A faint fear trembled through her as she faced off with her captor. "I know you're calling the shots, Jacob, but I have to think about the well-being of my students. It would be better for their mental health to focus on some work."

"I think it's best if you shut up and sit down," he replied.

Annalise remained standing. "The girls need to do something besides just sit against the wall for another day." It suddenly seemed vitally important that she stand her ground.

He gazed at her for a long moment. She boldly maintained eye contact with him. He finally looked away and frowned. "Can they work and be quiet? I don't want any damned noise."

"They can be very quiet," Annalise replied. She quickly turned to the girls. "Go to your computers," she said.

Thankfully they all moved quietly, eagerly to their desks. Jacob watched them. "Hey, Sadie, a little bird told me you're the smartest girl in this room."

"I am smart," Sadie replied. There was no pride in her voice, rather it was just a statement of fact.

"I heard you really know your way around computers," he said.

"Sometimes I think I might be smarter in computer arts than Miss Annalise," Sadie replied with pride, and flashed a small smile to her teacher.

"Yep, that's what the little bird told me," Jacob said.

"What's the name of your little bird?" Annalise asked. Had somebody on the inside told him how smart Sadie was? Was there somebody else involved in all this? Who from inside the school would have anything to do with this madness?

"The name is none of your business," he snapped. "I gave into them working at their desks, now stop asking me questions."

"Why don't you all build your own web page," Annalise said to the girls. "I want it to be a happy page with links to your favorite foods and animals and anything else that you love."

As the girls got to work, Annalise sat at her desk. Even though she knew in the grand scheme of things nothing had really changed, this felt like another success to her.

She wondered if Jacob had really had inside information on how bright Sadie was, or if he'd merely picked her out because she'd interacted with him and the other girls hadn't.

She didn't know, and at the moment it didn't matter. All that really mattered was that the girls were engaged in their work instead of sitting against a wall with nothing to think about but their own fear.

At least now, hopefully, they were thinking about their skills and creativity.

As the girls continued to work, she heard Evan on the bullhorn. He was attempting to build a relationship with Jacob, but the cult leader was having nothing to do with it. He would curse and demand Evan move the police presence away. He would then fire his gun out the window.

Meanwhile, as the girls worked, Gretchen walked between the desks, apparently checking to make sure the girls did nothing to contact anyone from the outside world. She occasionally asked questions to different girls, and it was obvious when they answered that the students were all terrified of her.

By noon Evan wasn't talking to Jacob anymore, but rather directed his comments to the men in the building. He told them that he understood and supported their mission of feeding the hungry and that he wanted a peaceful resolve to all of this.

Annalise knew Evan was using all the tools in his box to get to the men with Jacob. Unfortunately some of the attributes that make him a great hostage negotiator were also the traits that had eventually torn apart their relationship.

He'd been controlling and often emotionally unavailable to her during the time they had been together. She'd loved him desperately…still had deep feelings for him, but she hadn't been able to live with his control of her. She believed he'd seen her as too weak and too inadequate to run her own life. Not that any of that mattered now.

The standoff continued. Annalise knew at some point Evan was going to have to make a decision as far as ending this. If they used force to enter the building, she prayed that Jacob and his men would just put their hands up and surrender.

But there was no way to predict exactly what Jacob might do. There was no question that he appeared to grow more and more angry and agitated and quick to fire his gun as the minutes ticked by.

The girls seemed to have grown accustomed to Jacob firing his gun. When it happened, they no longer screamed or cried.

Jacob left the room often, and she could hear him yelling at his men. She had a feeling Evan's tactics were definitely getting to them.

She was more than ready to get out of here with her students. She just didn't know if Jacob and his deranged wife, Gretchen, would allow this to come to a peaceful end.

ANOTHER DAY WAS slowly drawing to an end. Evan was not only frustrated, but also his throat was sore and slightly husky from all the talking he'd done that day.

He lifted the bullhorn to his mouth once again. "Jacob, how about you let me come in there and have a one-on-one conversation with you. I'll come in unarmed and we can talk face-to-face."

"Just you?" Jacob yelled back.

Hope filled Evan. "Just me," he replied. If he

could get inside and talk to the man face-to-face, he was sure he could convince Jacob to give up.

"Step out where I can see you," Jacob said.

This certainly wouldn't be the first time Evan had entered a building to talk to a hostage taker, but he'd never gone in to speak to one who was so volatile and unpredictable. He stepped out from behind the patrol car and walked forward.

He took only a couple of steps when Jacob told him to halt.

"I'm going to lay down my gun," Evan said. With one hand up in the air, he used his other hand to unfasten the shoulder holster holding his gun. When he was finished, he laid it on the ground in front of him and then raised both hands above his head. "I'm unarmed and I'm coming in."

He took two steps forward and was about to take another when Jacob fired. Thankfully, the bullets kicked up the ground to the left and didn't hit him. Evan cursed, grabbed his gun and then scurried back behind the patrol car.

Jacob laughed. "Sorry, I changed my mind. I got nothing to say to you."

"Are you okay?" Nick asked Evan once he was back to safety.

"I'm fine." He released a deep breath. "If he'd wanted to kill me, he could have. I was an easy target."

"He's crazy," Nick replied.

"Crazy like a fox."

"Too bad Dr. Larsen couldn't identify what the trigger was for all this," Nick said.

Dr. Melinda Larsen was a criminal profiler. She was an attractive woman who was a specialist in reading body language for the FBI. Evan had contacted her to get a more thorough profile on Jacob Noble.

Her assessment was that Jacob was a narcissist who thrived on chaos. One of his teachings was that in the coming years food sources would dry up and only the wealthy would be able to feed themselves, thus building an "us versus them" mind-set in his followers.

He had set himself up as a godlike leader who would keep his followers safe and fed as things crumbled in society.

According to the information Hendrick had been able to give Dr. Larsen, she also believed Jacob used a combination of fear and unpredictability to control cult members.

It had been that unpredictability that he'd just shown, only in this case it was to prove to his followers that he was still in control and could make the FBI jump.

He raised the bullhorn. "I'm talking to the men inside the school. You have no way out of here. Jacob has led you into a corner where there is no escape. It's time to give up. This is a dead end, and if you don't surrender, then this will not end well."

He paused a moment and then spoke again. "At least let the hostages go."

The sun was dipping lower in the horizon, casting everything in shadows. He started to raise the bullhorn once again but paused as a tall man stood in the entrance of the school.

"Everyone hold your fire…hold your fire," he yelled to his men.

"If you're coming out, put your hands up over your head," he said to the man. "Get your hands up and walk out slowly."

The man hesitated for a long moment and then took one tentative step out of the building and raised his hands toward the sky. "Don't shoot," he said. "I'm unarmed. Please don't shoot me."

"Just walk forward slowly and keep your hands up over your head," Evan instructed. The air snapped with tension, and nobody else in the area spoke a word. For the first time since he'd arrived on scene, hope buoyed up in Evan. If this man walked out, then maybe the others would follow.

"Keep walking," Evan said. "You're doing fine. Just come straight forward, walk toward the sound of my voice."

The man took baby steps, and it was obvious he was afraid. He kept his arms over his head, but they shook with nerves. "Please don't shoot," he said again. "Please…please don't shoot me."

"Nobody is going to shoot you," Evan assured him. "Identify yourself."

"My name is Tim… Timothy Summers."

"Okay, Tim. You're doing great."

The man continued to move forward tiny step by

tiny step. He got halfway between the school building and the TCD team when gunfire filled the air.

Evan muttered a curse. "Hold your fire. Hold your damn fire," he yelled even as Tim screamed out in pain and then fell face-first to the ground.

It was then Evan realized it wasn't his men shooting, but rather Jacob or somebody from inside the school. "Cover me, cover me," Evan yelled.

As his men began to return fire, Evan grabbed a helmet, and crouching, he raced for the injured man, unmindful of any personal danger. All he saw was a human being who desperately needed help.

As he ran, a steady barrage of gunfire came from his men, providing him the cover he needed. The air filled with the acrid smoke from the blazing guns.

When Evan reached Tim, he wasn't conscious and his legs and back were riddled with gunshot wounds. He was bleeding badly. Evan grabbed him beneath his shoulders and began to pull him back toward safety.

Davis rushed to them and helped get the man behind the police line. The gunshots stopped and an eerie silence fell over the site.

"We need to get him into the ambulance right away," Davis said.

Evan motioned for the EMTs who were standing by with an ambulance, and they got the wounded man loaded on a gurney. Minutes later the emergency vehicle pulled away with sirens screaming.

"I doubt he's going to make it," Davis said grimly. "He took a lot of bullets."

"Damn it!" Evan exclaimed. He stared toward the brick building as an icy chill filled him. Jacob—or somebody in there—had just shot one of their own. The odds just got worse that Annalise and those girls were going to get out of there alive.

ANNALISE'S HEART BEAT so fast she thought she was going to pass out. The amount of gunfire…the sound of a man screaming from outside and Jacob cursing and firing his weapon out the window had scared not only the children, but also her.

Something had happened…something bad, but she didn't know what it was or what it might mean for these precious girls and herself.

They were all back against the wall for the night after spending the day working at their desks. When Jacob stormed out of the room, Annalise raced for her phone. Her fingers trembled as she texted Evan, asking what had just happened.

Annalise tried to keep it together for the girls, but tears raced down her cheeks. She was frightened, and she wanted her students to be anywhere but here.

After several minutes she received a text back from Evan, telling her that everything was okay. He said that there had been an exchange of gunfire, and one of Jacob's men was shot. He once again told her to stay strong and that he was doing all he could to get them out.

She quickly wiped away her tears, not only for herself, but also for the four girls holed up next to her and terrified. She had to stay strong for herself, but more so she had to stay strong for her students.

She heard Jacob's voice getting closer to the room, and she quickly disconnected from the phone and slid it beneath her thigh.

"They're either with me or against me," Jacob yelled as he and Gretchen stormed back into the room. "And if they're against me, then they will all pay the price."

He paced back and forth in front of the girls. "I won't stand for traitors. I won't stand for it."

"Calm down, Jacob. You're still the man in control," Gretchen said.

Jacob stopped in front of Annalise. "What's that?"

Annalise looked down and to her horror saw that the last rays of light coming in through the window shone off the edge of her cell phone that hadn't been tucked completely under her thigh. She froze, her heart beating fast and furiously.

"Yeah, what is that?" Gretchen leaned over and grabbed the cell phone. "What have we here?" She backhanded Annalise, the blow causing Annalise's head to hit the wall behind her. Her ears rang and her face stung from the blow.

"Stop it!" Sadie exclaimed. "Don't hurt her. Please Mr. Jacob, don't let her hurt Miss Annalise."

"Hush, Sadie," Annalise said, not wanting their anger turned on the child.

"I should shoot you," Gretchen said, her pale blue eyes cold as ice.

"Give me the phone," Jacob said. "Let's see who she's been talking to."

Annalise's heart continued to pound as Jacob thumbed through her messages. Thankfully most of her interaction with Evan had been by phone and FaceTime, and there was no recording of those.

Jacob dropped the phone to the floor and then ground it beneath the heel of his boot. All the while his dark eyes remained locked on Annalise.

Her breath caught in her chest, and every muscle in her body tensed. The girls were crying on either side of her, and she felt like throwing up as she waited for her consequences.

"I just shot a traitor," Jacob said with eyes narrowed.

"Let me take her out," Gretchen said. "I don't like her."

"You don't even know me," Annalise replied, pleased by the strength in her voice.

"I don't want to know you." She turned to her husband. "She's just another one of those girls who looked down on me all my life."

Jacob frowned. "We got more important things to do. Go check in with the men. And you," he said to Annalise. "Shut those girls up."

Annalise breathed a sigh of relief as Gretchen left the room. She quickly shushed the girls as her heartbeat resumed a more normal pace.

Within minutes complete darkness claimed the room. Jacob left the classroom and could be heard down the hallway talking loudly with his men.

Something was going to happen. Annalise could feel it in her bones, but she couldn't guess what it might be. Were they all finally going to give up?

She desperately wanted that to happen. She wanted them to give up peacefully. She wanted the girls to be out of here. She wished she had her phone. Evan had stopped talking on the bullhorn, and she wondered if he was planning to storm the building.

Being cut off from the outside world—from Evan—was terrifying as the night deepened and the tension inside of the school grew more intense. Jacob returned to his chair, and men came in and out of the room and whispered feverishly with him.

The girls finally fell asleep and Annalise closed her eyes, as well. Her thoughts went to the girls on either side of her. Emily was a sweet girl who was always the first to give a hug or offer encouragement to others. Tanya was a jokester and loved to make her friends giggle. Amanda was quiet and thoughtful. Then, of course, there was Sadie, who was not only sweet and giving, but also wise beyond her age.

How traumatized were they going to be by this event? Would they get out of here unscathed only to suffer from anxiety and or PTSD for the rest of their lives? Would Tanya lose her sense of humor forever? Would Emily withdraw from everyone? And what about Sadie, who had already been through so much in her short life?

Hopefully Regina Sandhurst would be willing to spend whatever money necessary on some therapy for her star students. These girls not only needed to survive the night, but also they needed to thrive in their lives going forward in spite of this horrifying event.

She had almost fallen asleep when gunfire snapped her eyes wide open and sent her heart racing. It wasn't just Jacob firing out the window in their room, it sounded like everyone in the building was shooting all at the same time. The girls screaming added to the cacophony of noise.

Within minutes smoke began to fill the air, coming in from the hallway. What was happening? Was the Brotherhood trying to kill all the police officers outside? Her heartbeat banged so erratically she wondered if she was about to have a heart attack. What was going on?

Gretchen ran into the room. "Let's go," she screamed at Jacob. "We have a chance if we move right now. It's time to go." To Annalise's horror, she yanked Sadie up by her arm.

"Leave her alone," Annalise yelled. She struggled to her feet and tried to get Sadie away from Gretchen. "Let go of her," she screamed as she held tight to Sadie's other arm.

"Let her go," Gretchen yelled as she tugged Sadie closer to her. "I swear before this is all over I'm going to kill you."

"I'm not letting go," Annalise replied feverishly. She couldn't let Gretchen take Sadie. She tried to pull the little girl closer to her.

Gretchen punched Annalise in the stomach hard. Her breath whooshed out of her, and pain weakened her knees. Still, she reached out and grabbed one of Gretchen's braids and held tight.

The woman screamed and grabbed Annalise's wrist. As long as Gretchen had one hand holding Sadie and the other holding Annalise, she couldn't get to the gun in her waistband.

Annalise yanked as hard as she could on the woman's hair. Gretchen screamed again in outrage. Jacob rushed them both, and shoved Annalise so hard her back smashed against the wall and she lost her grip on Sadie and Gretchen. "No," she screamed. Jacob swung the child up over his broad shoulder, and then he and his wife ran out of the room.

Chapter Six

Annalise struggled to her feet, half breathless and nauseous from the blow she had taken to the stomach and the force of her back slamming into the wall. She had no idea what was going on. All she knew was she desperately needed to get Sadie back.

She ran out into the hallway, but she saw no sign of them. *Oh, God, where had they gone?* The smoke grew thicker, and she narrowed her eyes against it. She coughed as it burned the back of her throat.

Was the building on fire? She felt no heat radiating from anywhere. She didn't believe there was a fire threat. She suspected it came from a smoke bomb. And that meant the people outside were taking the building by storm.

It all seemed surreal…the smoke, the gunshots… the terror. When she heard the cries of the other three girls, she ran back into the classroom.

"Come on, girls. You need to get up. I want you to get beneath the desks. Duck and cover." Unsure what to expect, she only hoped the desks would provide the girls some measure of safety against whatever was happening.

It felt like the apocalypse, like the entire world was exploding all around them. The sound of shattering glass added to the chaos. The girls continued to cry as they huddled beneath the desks.

Again Annalise looked out into the hallway. Where was Sadie? Where had they taken her and for what reason? Would they be back to take the other girls? Maybe she should move the girls out of here.

She stepped back into the classroom, intending to do just that when the gunfire suddenly halted. The only sound was that of men yelling for help.

"Annalise!" Evan's voice rose above the pandemonium. It came from somewhere just outside the room.

"In here," she cried desperately. "Evan, we're in here."

Then he was there, standing right in front of her, and she was in his arms. "They took Sadie," she cried. "You have to find her. Evan, they took her and then ran out of the room."

"Gretchen hit Miss Annalise in the stomach," Emily said.

"And Jacob pushed her real hard and she fell back," Amanda added.

Evan looked at her in alarm. "I'm okay. You just need to find Sadie," she replied.

He released her and got on his radio, which was attached to the top of his shoulder. Annalise gathered the girls close to her side and prayed that the good guys outside had Jacob and Gretchen in custody and Sadie was safe somewhere out of the school building.

Evan got off his radio and drew all of them closer to him. "We're going to get the girls to go out through the window."

As he said the words, another man appeared outside the window. He knocked out what was left of the jagged glass, and Evan hunched down in front of the girls.

"That man at the window is Davis and he's with Nick, another agent. They are going to carry you all to safety."

Annalise hurried the girls to the window, where Evan raised Tanya and passed her out the window. He did the same with the other two girls.

"Is Sadie safe?" Annalise asked worriedly. "Do they have her someplace safe outside?"

"Let's get you out of here," he replied. He grabbed her hand, and she squeezed his tightly.

They left the classroom and immediately she understood why he had taken the girls out the window. Chaos reigned in the hallway. Several wounded men cried out as paramedics and other emergency personnel attended to them.

Evan dropped her hand and instead threw his arm around her shoulders and pulled her closer as they maneuvered their way around the wounded and then stepped out of the building.

Free. She was finally free. She breathed in the cool night air, but her relief in being out of the school only lasted a moment. "Evan, where is Sadie? Jacob and Gretchen grabbed her and took off with her. Did somebody catch them? Is she okay?"

Evan took her by the arm and led her toward an awaiting ambulance. "I don't need any medical care," she protested. She stopped walking and faced him. "I just need to know if Sadie is safe." Worry flooded her veins. Why wasn't he telling her anything about Sadie?

"Annalise, look, we still have a situation here." A pulse throbbed in his strong jawline. "Jacob and Gretchen managed to get away, and they have Sadie with them."

"My God." Annalise nearly fell to the ground in horror. How on earth had they gotten away and why had they taken Sadie with them? Despite the chaos of the scene surrounding them, her brain now whirled with all the things that had happened between Sadie and Jacob.

Before she could speak, an attractive woman with long dark hair approached them. "This is Rowan. She'll see to it that you get the medical attention you need and get home safely," Evan said. "Somebody will be in contact with you to arrange to take your statement at a later time."

"I'm not going home," Annalise protested vehemently. "I... I think he took Sadie because, despite her age, she is a computer genius. I know if she gets anywhere near a computer she'll contact me. We... we have a secret page set up and a secret language."

She grabbed Evan's forearm. "I know she'll try to contact me, and she'll help us rescue her."

He stared at her. "What makes you think he took her for her computer skills?" he asked.

"He knew she was the smartest on the computer. I... I think he had some inside information about her." Evan looked at her sharply as she continued. "I think they came into the school specifically to take Sadie, but the police arrived too quickly for them to get out. If I'm right about all this, then I can help. Evan, I'm not going home."

He hesitated, frowned and rubbed the back of his neck. "Okay," he finally relented. He then looked at Rowan once again. "Let the paramedics take a look at her wounds and then bring her to the hotel and arrange a room for her and a meal, and make sure she has a computer. I have to go." Without another word he turned away and headed into the center of the chaos.

"Annalise, let's go," Rowan said gently, and she touched the teacher's shoulder.

On the short drive to the hotel, all Annalise could think of was Sadie with her big blue eyes and happy smile. What exactly did Jacob want from her? There was little doubt in Annalise's mind that Sadie had been taken because of her computer skills, so what did they want her to do? And if she did what was asked of her, would she be killed afterward?

"I'm sure you're exhausted," Rowan said minutes later as she opened the door to room 110 of a hotel close to the school.

"I just want Sadie to be found and returned safe and sound," Annalise replied. "I… I was supposed to protect her. It was my job to protect her and I failed." Tears blurred her vision.

To her surprise Rowan put her arms around Annalise and hugged her. "You did everything in your power, Annalise. You did an amazing job in keeping those girls safe in a dangerous situation. Don't beat yourself up."

Rowan finally released her and then stepped away. "I'll be right back with a computer for you to use."

When she left the room, Annalise stared around her. The hotel room was serviceable, with a king-size bed covered by a light blue spread, and a dresser and a television. A desk and a small round table sat in a corner.

Rowan returned with a laptop and carried it to the desk. "This should work for you," she said, taking a moment to power it up. "I'll go get you something to eat. I know you've been existing on next to nothing for the last couple of days. Is there anything special you'd like?"

"I'm not really hungry," Annalise replied. She didn't want to even think about food when Sadie was missing, kidnapped by a deranged man and his sadistic wife.

She sat in the desk chair and opened up the laptop. She quickly connected to the internet and went to the page she'd set up just for her and her students to use.

Tears once again blurred her vision. Sadie had been so incredibly brave throughout the entire ordeal, and she had stayed strong throughout the passing days and nights. Annalise prayed she would continue to be brave and strong wherever she was at the moment.

Was Sadie going to get a meal? Would Jacob and Gretchen make sure she had food? When the two adults fed their own faces, would they remember to feed Sadie?

She hadn't expected to see anything from Sadie so soon on the page, and there wasn't anything there yet. She drew in a deep breath and released it slowly.

Evan. Seeing him again, even for only a few moments, had stirred something deep inside her. But there were so many other crazy emotions racing through her right now it was difficult to sort it all out.

Had she been so happy to see him simply because he represented safety and her freedom? Or was there still something there, something that yearned for what might have been with him.

She released another deep breath. Hopefully Evan and his men would find Jacob and Gretchen soon and bring Sadie back to safety.

"I should have fought harder," she murmured to herself as she thought about that moment when Gretchen had grabbed Sadie. It had been so unexpected. However, somehow, someway she should have fought much harder and never let them take her.

It was difficult for her to realize it was Friday

night. Thankfully Evan had gotten them out of there in just a little over forty-eight hours. If Chief Cummings had continued to be in charge of the situation, who knew when they might have gotten out. Who knew if they would have even survived?

She hadn't realized Rowan had gone to get her food until she returned with several sacks from the local diner. "I wasn't sure what you'd like," Rowan said as she began to unload the items onto the table. "There's a salad and some chicken noodle soup. I also brought you a few personal items like a new hairbrush and a toothbrush and toothpaste and a change of clothing."

Despite Annalise's worry, the scent of the food was heavenly. "Thank you for everything, and I guess I am hungry after all. That soup smells really good."

"Eat and then try to get some rest. You've been through a terrible ordeal," Rowan said.

"It's not over yet," Annalise replied darkly. "It won't be over until Sadie is safe and sound. Where are the other girls now?"

"They are currently in the hospital being treated for dehydration and getting other medical treatment they might require. Their resident attendants are with them, and they're all doing just fine," Rowan assured her.

"What about Belinda? Do you know how she is?"

"She immediately went in for emergency surgery and is now in serious, but stable condition. She should be just fine, thanks to you. It's a good thing you got her out when you did. Now, I need to get back to the school. Are you going to be okay here alone?"

"I'm good," Annalise replied. "All I really want is for Sadie to be found."

"I'm sure the team is working very hard to find her and the two fugitives," Rowan replied. "Do you need anything else?"

"No, you've been more than kind," Annalise replied.

"Then let's hope the next time I talk with you will be when Sadie is safe and the bad guys are behind bars." Then with a quick goodbye Rowan left.

At least Annalise could rest assured that the other three girls were being well taken care of. All of the girls at the school were very close to their resident attendants and looked to them for emotional support. The resident attendants were good at loving and supporting their young charges.

She stared at the computer screen even as she moved from the chair at the desk to a chair at the table. From there she could still see if anything popped up on the internet page while she ate.

The salad tasted fresh and good, and then she dove into the hearty delicious soup. Once she was full and her mind had finally slowed down from the chaos of the past couple of days, her thoughts once again filled with Evan.

Did she want to see him again so badly because she hoped he had news about Sadie? Absolutely.

But, there was also a small part of her that wanted to reconnect with him after the ordeal.

Still, what she wanted more than anything was for him to tell her that Jacob and Gretchen were behind bars and Sadie was safe and with her resident attendant.

"DAMN IT, HOW did this happen?" Evan yelled in a rage as he glared at Chief Cummings. "How in the hell did your men allow this to happen?"

When the dust had settled, Evan was told that the black van that had been parked behind the school was gone. Jacob had apparently driven it right through the police line and had gotten away.

"My men did what they could, but somebody was shooting through one of the van windows," Chief Cummings replied defensively.

"What did they do? Did they just run into the woods and hide instead of returning fire? If nothing else, why in the hell didn't somebody think to shoot out the tires so they couldn't drive away?"

"I'm sure they tried," Chief Cummings replied. "I pulled a lot of my men off the guard duty at the back of the school. Some of them needed a break, and others I reassigned to regular patrol duty."

"Right, because it was more important to ticket jaywalkers?" Evan asked incredulously.

"You said I had the right to reassign some of my men," Chief Cummings protested.

"Nevertheless, nobody from inside the school should have had a chance to get into that van, let

"One Minute" Survey

You get TWO books and TWO Mystery Gifts...

YOU pick your books –
WE pay for everything.
You get TWO new books and TWO Mystery Gifts...
absolutely FREE!
Total retail value: Over $20!

Dear Reader,

Your opinions are important to us. So if you'll participate in our fast and free "One Minute" Survey, **YOU** can pick two wonderful books that **WE** pay for!

As a leading publisher of women's fiction, we'd love to hear from you. That's why we promise to reward you for completing our survey.

IMPORTANT: Please complete the survey and return it. We'll send your Free Books and Free Mystery Gifts right away. **And we pay for shipping and handling too!**

↖ *We pay for EVERYTHING!*

Thank you again for participating in our "One Minute" Survey. It really takes just a minute (or less) to complete the survey... and your free books and gifts will be well worth it!

Sincerely,

Pam Powers

Pam Powers
for Reader Service

"One Minute" Survey

GET YOUR FREE BOOKS AND FREE GIFTS!

✓ Complete this Survey ✓ Return this survey

◄ **DETACH AND MAIL CARD TODAY!** ▼

1 Do you try to find time to read every day?

☐ YES ☐ NO

2 Do you prefer stories with suspenseful storylines?

☐ YES ☐ NO

3 Do you enjoy having books delivered to your home?

☐ YES ☐ NO

4 Do you find a Larger Print size easier on your eyes?

☐ YES ☐ NO

YES! I have completed the above "One Minute" Survey. Please send me my Two Free Books and Two Free Mystery Gifts (worth over $20 retail). I understand that I am under no obligation to buy anything, as explained on the back of this card.

❏ I prefer the regular-print edition
182/382 HDL GNSS

❏ I prefer the larger-print edition
199/399 HDL GNSS

FIRST NAME | LAST NAME

ADDRESS

APT.# | CITY

STATE/PROV. | ZIP/POSTAL CODE

READER SERVICE—Here's how it works:

Accepting your 2 free Harlequin Intrigue® books and 2 free gifts (gifts valued at approximately $10.00 retail) places you under no obligation to buy anything. You may keep the books and gifts and return the shipping statement marked "cancel." If you do not cancel, about a month later we'll send you 6 additional books and bill you just $4.99 each for the regular-print edition or $5.99 each for the larger-print edition in the U.S. or $5.74 each for the regular-print edition or $6.49 each for the larger-print edition in Canada. That is a savings of at least 13% off the cover price. It's quite a bargain! Shipping and handling is just 50¢ per book in the U.S. and $1.25 per book in Canada*. You may cancel at any time, but if you choose to continue, every month we'll send you 6 more books, which you may either purchase at the discount price plus shipping and handling or return to us and cancel your subscription. *Terms and prices subject to change without notice. Prices do not include sales taxes which will be charged (if applicable) based on your state or country of residence. Canadian residents will be charged applicable taxes. Offer not valid in Quebec. Books received may not be as shown. All orders subject to approval. Credit or debit balances in a customer's account(s) may be offset by any other outstanding balance owed by or to the customer. Please allow 3 to 4 weeks for delivery. Offer available while quantities last.

▲ If offer card is missing write to: Reader Service, P.O. Box 1341, Buffalo, NY 14240-8531 or visit www.ReaderService.com ▲

BUSINESS REPLY MAIL
FIRST-CLASS MAIL   PERMIT NO. 717   BUFFALO, NY

POSTAGE WILL BE PAID BY ADDRESSEE

READER SERVICE
PO BOX 1341
BUFFALO NY 14240-8571

NO POSTAGE
NECESSARY
IF MAILED
IN THE
UNITED STATES

alone drive it off." Evan didn't wait for an answer. If he looked at Chief Cummings for one more minute, he was going to completely lose it.

Instead, he turned and headed toward the mobile vehicle. He couldn't believe the lack of professionalism that Chief Cummings had shown, or the lack of training the force had since they appeared to allow Jacob to just drive away, apparently with his wife and Sadie, as well.

Still, he'd known something was going down when the men in the school had all begun firing out the front school windows at the same time. It had been a coordinated assault, and Evan had known immediately that it had been a ruse for something else that might be happening.

Evan had already made the decision to go in, not trusting that Jacob was going to hold it together for another night. He'd instructed his men to prepare to move in so they were immediately ready to respond.

Flash-bang grenades and smoke bombs had disoriented the men inside enough to force them to surrender and make the assault on the school successful. Evan now realized Jacob had ordered all of his men to shoot through the front windows and provide the distraction so that he and his wife could make their escape out of the back of the school.

Evan's anger was rich and thick and filled his chest with an uncomfortable tightness. They now had two criminals on the run with a little girl as a hostage. Things had gone from bad to worse.

Was Annalise right? Had Sadie been taken because she was so gifted with her ability regarding computer science? Had Jacob had inside information about the students? Or had they taken her to use as a human shield if needed when they had escaped? If the latter was true, then they would probably dump Sadie the first chance they got. The real question was if they'd dump her dead or alive. The pressure in his chest increased.

"Hendrick," he said once he'd connected with the tech. "What have you got for me?"

"Not much. They must be traveling on back roads, and there are a hell of a lot of mountain roads without cameras in that area," Hendrick replied. "Since we don't know what direction they fled, I'm watching the available traffic cameras within a twenty-five-mile radius in each direction. But so far I've got nothing. I'll let you know the minute I do."

"I need you to also be on the lookout for any report of a child found," Evan said. "It's possible Sadie will be dumped on the side of the road somewhere if she's no longer useful to them." Hopefully, if that happened, they would dump her alive.

"Got it," Hendrick replied.

"Also, Annalise had a feeling Jacob had some inside information on the girls. I need you to do thorough background checks on all the employees and see what you find."

"I'm on it."

As Evan disconnected, Nick stuck his head in the doorway. "Hey, man, we've got a live one out here. He's not hurt and he's singing like a bird."

Maybe they would finally get some answers that had eluded them so far. Evan followed Nick to the back of a patrol car where a tall, blond-haired, handcuffed man stood. "I'm Special Agent Evan Duran," he said to the prisoner. "What's your name?"

"Ben... Ben Hanson. This...this all wasn't supposed to be like this." He looked utterly shellshocked. "This is the very last thing we all wanted."

"So, what exactly did you want when you came into the school?" Evan asked. "Why are you here?"

"We were supposed to get in, grab one of the genius students and then get out. We didn't intend to fire a shot. There wasn't supposed to be a standoff. Nobody was ever supposed to get hurt."

"So, what made it go south?" Evan asked.

"First of all Jacob told us nobody would be in the school except a teacher and a few of her students. Somebody panicked and started shooting. Then I guess the security guard managed to ring the alarm and the cops started showing up way before we expected."

"What did you want with the student?" Evan asked.

Ben frowned. "Jacob said the kids in the school were smart enough to break into the World Bank. He said when that happened there would be all kinds of financial chaos, and during that pandemonium he'd transfer enough money to distribute to the poor and hungry. We all knew it was illegal, but we believed it was for the greater good. He said we would help to stop hunger all over the world."

"Did you all know that Jacob and his wife own some property in the Caymen Islands along with a healthy bank account in their names only?"

Ben stared at him for a long moment and then slowly shook his head and released a deep, bitter laugh. "I don't know why that should surprise me now. In the end they only saved their own skins and left the rest of us here to die. He even fired at Tim. He shot him in the back when he was giving himself up."

Ben's eyes filled with tears. "I saw the ambulance pull away after he got shot. Is…is he okay?"

"He didn't make it," Nick said curtly. Evan knew Nick had gotten the information from the hospital. Despite Evan's and Davis's best efforts to save the man, he had been DOA.

Ben's eyes glazed over with emotion. "Damn Jacob for killing him. We thought Jacob was a great leader for change in society, but he turned out to be nothing more than a greedy monster."

"What was the plan? Where was Jacob planning on taking the child?" Evan asked.

"The plan was for all of us to return to the compound, but now I have no idea where they might have gone."

"Has Jacob or Gretchen ever talked about any other property they own?" Evan asked. "Does anyone close to them own someplace where they might go?"

Ben shook his head. "As far as I know, neither of them had any family. None of us own any property.

If anyone had any, we all sold it and donated the proceeds to the group before we moved into the compound with Jacob. I've never heard either of them talk about any property they might own, especially a place in the Caymen Islands," he finished bitterly.

Evan sighed in frustration and turned to Nick. "Go ahead and get him processed and out of here."

Everything that could be done was being done. His men were processing the crime scene, and Jacob's thugs had been rounded up. The wounded were being attended to, and officials all over the area were looking for the black panel van. Law enforcement at all the nearby airports was also on the lookout for the fugitives.

Maybe Annalise was right and somehow Sadie would manage to contact them and be able to tell them where she was. With this thought in mind, he decided to head to the hotel.

As Rowan drove him to the room his head filled with thoughts of Annalise. Seeing her again, even so briefly, had been surprisingly good and difficult at the same time.

He was relieved she was safe, but he couldn't be content until Sadie was also safe. Right now, Annalise was a means to that end.

"Try to get some rest," Rowan said as she pulled up in front of the hotel. "I know things aren't resolved yet, but you can't keep pushing yourself like you've been doing since you got here. You need to take time to sleep and recharge, otherwise you'll end up being no good to anyone."

"I know," he replied. Just that quickly a thick blanket of exhaustion fell over him. He tried to shrug it off as he got out of the car, but he was only half-successful.

She handed him a room key. "You're in room 108 and Annalise is in room 110."

"Got it," he replied.

"I'll be back with some food for you," Rowan said. "And I'll arrange for a rental car, too."

"Sounds good," he replied, and then braced himself for seeing Annalise again. He knocked on her hotel room door.

"Come in."

He was surprised to find her door unlocked. He pushed open the door and stepped inside. She stood from the chair at the desk and faced him. There was a charged stillness between them for a long moment.

She moved forward and into his waiting arms. She'd just been through a horrendous event. Who knew what she'd had to do to survive her time in that classroom.

He held her as she buried her face in the crook of his neck and cried. He knew her tears were a combination of exhaustion and stress, and fear for the little girl who was still missing.

He caressed a hand up and down her back and murmured soothing sounds as he waited for her to stop crying. He wanted to be here for her, but he also needed her to move away from him.

Holding her was bringing up old memories he shouldn't entertain. Besides, he still had an active crime to resolve, and that's where all his thoughts and the last of his energy needed to go.

Finally she gathered her emotions, and after drawing several deep, shuddery breaths, she stepped back from him and sat on the edge of the bed. "Any news on Sadie?"

He turned to close and lock her door, then faced her once again. "Not yet. We're doing everything possible to find them, but so far we have nothing." He gestured toward the computer. "You said Sadie might try to get you a message, and let's hope that happens soon. One of Jacob's men confirmed that was their plan all along, to take one of the girls and break into a banking system. I'd send you home, but you also mentioned a secret language you all have."

She tucked a strand of her long hair behind her ear, an old nervous habit he remembered from years past. "It was mostly just for fun. The girls loved learning it and using it to communicate with me and each other. For me it was just another tool to keep their minds engaged and challenged."

"So, do you really think Sadie will try to contact you on this page?"

"Absolutely. If she gets an opportunity to get on a computer, then I believe she'll make contact. She's very smart, Evan." Tears glistened in her beautiful green eyes once again. "She's very special, and she's already been through a lot in her short life."

"We'll get her back, Annalise," he said. There was no question that Jacob and his wife were dangerous criminals, but at the moment they needed Sadie to go through with their insane plan.

"You mentioned something about thinking Jacob had inside information?"

She frowned thoughtfully. "I can't be absolutely sure, but all my instincts say yes. Jacob knew Sadie was the smartest of the girls. He told her that a little bird had told him she was the smartest. At one point he offered her something to eat and not the others. He also said something about having information that the only people who would be in the school when they burst in would be me and a few students."

"That definitely sounds like there was an insider working with them." He grimaced. "I've got Hendrick checking into the backgrounds of everyone who works at the school. Is there anyone you can think of who might be a part of this?"

Her frown deepened. "I can't imagine anyone I work with helping those monsters. I truly believe all the teachers love their jobs and the students, and would never have anything to do with what happened."

"I know you must be exhausted. Why don't you take a shower and then sleep for a couple of hours? I'll stay here and keep an eye on the web page, and I'll wake you if anything shows up there," he suggested.

She looked down at herself and frowned and nodded in agreement. He knew Rowan had provided fresh clothing for her as well as some toiletries.

"A hot shower sounds wonderful. Maybe I can

wash off some of the filth I feel after being around those horrible people."

She picked up the things Rowan had gotten for her and then headed for the bathroom. Once she was gone and the door had closed behind her, he sank down on the edge of the bed and drew in several deep breaths.

The sound of the shower running instantly evoked a vision of her beautiful naked body beneath the water. He closed his eyes. They used to love to shower together.

He opened his eyes and released another deep sigh. He'd worked many difficult cases in his years with TCD, but to save a little girl in danger by working with the ex-lover who had walked out on him promised to be one of his most challenging ever.

Chapter Seven

The long hot shower refreshed Annalise more than she wanted to admit under the circumstances, but it didn't completely wash away the trauma of the entire event. Her lower lip was still slightly swollen from the slaps she'd received, and her body ached from the various bouts of physical abuse she'd endured from Gretchen.

Still, she'd take the aches and pain. At least she was alive, and she prayed that Sadie would be recovered alive and well.

She pulled on the jeans and TCD tee Rowan had provided, and then stood in front of the vanity mirror and dried her long hair, trying not to think about Evan and their past relationship. That was over and done, and there was absolutely nothing between them now but the shared desire to save a little girl.

She mentally thanked Rowan for the personal items as she brushed her teeth, and by the time she was finished with the simple task, a deep weariness filled her.

The energy she'd expended over the ordeal had

been both mental and physical. She'd gotten very little sleep during the days and nights in captivity, and the continuous stream of adrenaline she'd endured while in that classroom resulted in a bone weariness she could no longer fight off.

"Anything?" she asked as she stepped out of the bathroom.

"Nothing so far," Evan replied. He was seated at the table eating a large sandwich. "The only thing that happened while you were showering is that Rowan got me some food."

She sat on the edge of the bed. "Rowan's an angel."

"She is, and she's really smart, too. She handles all aspects of the ground game. I swear if she hadn't gotten between me and the chief of police several times, I might have shot him."

He explained some of the issues he'd had with the chief, and as he spoke she found her eyelids growing heavier and heavier. "Get some sleep, Annalise," he finally said. "You're too tired to even pretend to be listening to me."

"I'm listening," she protested sleepily.

He got up and turned off the light over the table, leaving only a small desk lamp illuminating the room. "I promise I'll wake you if something breaks," he told her.

"Okay." She stretched out on the bed without turning down the spread. It was so amazing to rest and know she was safe. Still, she offered up a prayer for Sadie.

"Hey," he called to her softly. "You were great in there."

She released a half laugh and a half sob of exhaustion.

"Annalise, are you sure you're okay?" he asked.

"I will be once Sadie is home," she replied drowsily.

"We'll get her," he murmured.

Almost immediately sleep claimed her. She slept hard and without dreams. She awakened to early-morning daylight drifting in through the parted curtains, and the scent of fresh coffee.

She bolted upright and her first thought was of Sadie. Evan sat at the table, his eyes red-rimmed and lines of exhaustion cut down the sides of his handsome face. "There's fresh coffee in the pot."

"Thanks. I guess you haven't heard anything?"

He shook his head, frowning. "Nothing. It's like they drove away from the school and disappeared off the face of the earth."

She raked her fingers through her hair and then got out of bed. She poured herself a cup of the hotel coffee and joined him at the table.

"Feel better?" he asked, although his gaze shot to someplace just over her head.

"Much better," she replied. "I certainly didn't mean to sleep as long as I did."

"I'm sure you needed it," he replied.

Evan looked tired. He wore a white shirt with sleeves rolled up to his elbows and dark pants. His hair was slightly mussed and his beard was growing out, but that did nothing to detract from how appealing he was.

She sipped her coffee as the silence grew between them. The parted curtains gave her a view of a swimming pool outside. She peeked out and then stared down into her coffee cup. She wasn't sure what to say, and she had a feeling he felt the same way about her.

Finally she gazed at him once again. "Evan, you look positively exhausted," she said. "I know you spent all your time on the bullhorn and working the scene, so maybe it's way past time you take a shower and get a little bit of sleep. I can watch the computer screen and let you know if anything happens."

He leaned back in the chair and took a drink of his coffee. "Yeah, I guess that might be a good idea. I'm definitely reaching the end of my energy."

"Evan, you won't be good for anything if you don't stop and take care of yourself," she chided.

"Maybe you could ring me in an hour or two so I don't sleep too long," he suggested.

"I'll have to use the house phone. Jacob destroyed my cell phone when he found it on me."

He looked at her for a long moment, his eyes narrowed. "What else did he do?"

She ran her tongue over her lower lip where the swelling was barely noticeable. "I don't want to talk about…"

"I'm sorry, Annalise. I'm sorry you had to endure that kind of abuse."

"It's over now. Isn't it time for you to get some sleep?"

He took another drink of his coffee and then stood. "If you're sure you've got this, then I'll head back to my room and take a short nap. My room is next door on the right, room 108."

"I've got this. Go get some rest."

"Close and lock the door behind me," he said.

When he left the room, she locked the door then resumed her seat at the table. "Sadie, where are you?" she whispered to herself as she stared at the computer screen.

If Jacob and Gretchen hadn't put her in front of a computer yet, maybe it was because they were still traveling and looking for a safe place to land. They had to know they couldn't go back to their compound, so it was anyone's guess where they might be going.

She sipped her coffee and her mind filled with the thought of Evan showering. A bit of tension coiled in her stomach, a tension that had nothing to do with Sadie or what was going on with the crimes.

She shook her head to dispel the memories. It had been nearly three years since they had been together as a couple. That amount of time changed people. She didn't really know him now.

She had no idea what he had done or who he might have loved since they'd been a couple. It was possible he had a meaningful other right now.

She didn't know what life experiences he'd had in

the time they'd been apart. There were things they hadn't shared. They were really virtual strangers now.

Still, there was no question being with him again had stirred some confusing emotions inside her, but she told herself all she wanted from him—all she really needed—was for him to bring Sadie home. Then they could both get back to their separate lives.

"Maria," Evan yelled to his little sister, who had just run into the alleyway chasing a butterfly. Reluctantly he got up from the stoop where he had been sitting with some of his buddies.

"Maria," he shouted once again. Sometimes watching his little sister could be a real pain.

He entered the alleyway, the smell of the overflowing garbage cans beneath the heat of the day pungent and nearly overpowering. He narrowed his eyes as he advanced deeper into the darker narrow passageway.

He suddenly froze. A man, wearing a dirty blue bandana to hide the lower half of his face, held Maria against his body with a knife to her throat. A terror he'd never known before ripped through Evan.

"Go on, get out of here, boy," the man said gruffly.

Maria's big brown eyes pleaded with Evan to do something, anything to save her.

On trembling legs he took two steps forward. "Let her go." Sweat trickled down the center of his back. Nausea rose in Evan's throat, and his entire

*body flushed in horror. This was like something out
of the scariest movie he'd ever seen. He had to do
something to save his little sister.*

*"I told you to get out of here unless you want me
to slit her throat," the man growled.*

"No, please don't hurt her!" Evan exclaimed.

*The man lunged forward and swiped the knife
toward Evan's face. Evan leaped backward as
the blade slashed perilously close to his cheek.
"Please...let her go. She's my sister."*

*"You aren't in control here, kid. She's mine now."
The man suddenly picked up Maria, then turned and
ran. "Evan," the little girl cried.*

"Maria!" Evan screamed.

EVAN BOLTED UPRIGHT, his heart racing and his body
bathed in a light sheen of sweat. For just a moment,
he was a frightened eight-year-old again and in that
foul-smelling alley, confronting a man with a knife
who had his little sister.

He wiped a hand down his face and then realized it hadn't been the nightmare that had ultimately
awakened him, but rather Hendrick on a video call.

He scrambled out of bed and hurried to the desk
where his computer was set up. "Hendrick, you have
something for me?"

"The van."

Evan straightened, now wide awake. "What
about it?"

"I found it."

"Where?"

"Believe it or not, in the parking lot of a grocery store five miles from the school," Hendrick replied. "I ran security tape in the lot, and it looked like Jacob, Gretchen and Sadie left the van and then walked out of camera range. Unfortunately, I haven't been able to pick them up on any other cameras in the area."

Evan cursed. "So, we don't have any idea what kind of vehicle they might be in now or where they might have gone."

"That's about the sum of it," Hendrick replied grimly.

"Is it possible they're on foot right now?"

Hendrick shook his head. "I don't believe so. They got out of that van with a sense of purpose. They didn't look around, but rather started walking quickly. I think they knew there was another ride waiting for them."

"Give me the exact location of the van," Evan said.

He took down the pertinent information and then disconnected. He grabbed his holster and gun from the nightstand and then left his room. He knocked on Annalise's door.

She opened the door. "Evan… I thought you were sleeping."

"I just got a call from Hendrick. He found the black van in a parking lot about five miles from here, so I'm calling some of the men to meet me there."

"I'm coming with you," she said. "Maybe Sadie

somehow left some kind of clue for us in the van. Just let me grab my room key card."

Evan had hoped after a couple hours of sleep he would be able to better focus on finding Sadie. Although he felt physically refreshed from the almost two hours of sleep he had gotten, mentally he still felt half-exhausted with the weight of the case on his shoulders and trying to deal with his unexpected emotions where Annalise was concerned.

Minutes later, with her seated next to him in the rental car, he had an overwhelming need to reach out and touch her.

He gripped the steering wheel more tightly. He had to stay focused on the crime that had brought them together in the first place and not on anything else. He still had a little girl to find, and he was desperate to get that right.

While he drove he called Nick and Davis and told them where the van was parked and instructed them to meet him there. He then called Hendrick to see if there had been any stolen car reports from the area in and around the parking lot.

"Already done," Hendrick replied, and so far there were no stolen car reports. "And I think it's safe to say that if they had stolen a car, it would have been reported by now. According to the time stamp on the security tape, they had to have driven directly from the school to that parking lot."

"It's possible Jacob arranged for somebody at the compound to meet him with a car. See if you can get in touch with whoever is in charge of the traffic in and out of the compound. Maybe they'll have a record of a car that went out sometime last night and then never came back."

"On it. I'll get back to you as soon as I have something."

Evan hung up his phone and glanced at his passenger. She looked as tense as he felt as he pulled into the grocery store's large parking lot. "The van is parked in section D," he said, slowing to find the right aisle.

"Over there," she said, and pointed to their left.

He turned and slowed down even more. He saw the vehicle right before Annalise pointed it out. There was an empty space next to it, and Evan pulled in and parked.

He and Annalise both jumped out of the car at the same time. He headed for the driver's side door and she went to the back door. The side of the van had a couple of bullet holes, and he was vaguely surprised to find it unlocked.

If the police officers who were tasked to keep the van from leaving the school had done their job right, then there would have been bullet holes in the front of the vehicle. The fact that they were on the sides told the whole story of incompetence that Evan had suspected, and it infuriated him.

He'd only just begun to search it when Nick and Davis arrived. He got out of the van and instructed Annalise to do the same. "I want you two to go over this with a fine-tooth comb. As you know, we're looking for anything that might indicate where they were going from here and what kind of vehicle they might be driving now."

As the two agents got busy checking out the van, Evan got back on his phone to check in with some of the others, including Chief Cummings. Everyone had a job to do, and it was Evan's job to coordinate all the efforts to find the fugitives.

Unfortunately, the fact that Annalise believed so strongly that Sadie would contact her by using some sort of code made her an important piece of this whole puzzle. She was especially important right now since they had absolutely no leads on where the three had gone or how they might be traveling.

Before he'd fallen asleep, he'd contacted Rowan to get Annalise a cell phone she could use for the time being. Annalise got on the phone and checked the secret page, then then shook her head. Apparently Sadie still hadn't made contact.

"Hey, I've got something here," Nick said from the backseat of the van. "It looks like something has been scratched into the back of the front seat."

Evan looked to where Nick pointed. Sure enough, it looked like a fingernail or something had been used to scratch letters, numbers and symbols that made no sense.

"Annalise, take a look at this and see what you think," he said. He backed out and gave her room to look.

She leaned in. "It's…it's from Sadie." Her voice was thick with emotion as she straightened. "It's in our secret language. It says 'Sadie was here.'" Her eyes filled with tears as she gazed at him. "She wanted me…she wanted everyone to know that she was here." She began to cry.

There was something particularly heartbreaking about a kidnapped little girl wanting her teacher and law enforcement to know that she was in the van, that she was still alive.

As Evan saw the emotion ripping through Annalise, he couldn't just stand by and watch. He pulled her into his arms and held her.

"I'm sorry," she said as she swiped her cheeks in obvious embarrassment. "I don't seem to have much control over my emotions right now."

"It's okay," he replied. "I'm sure you're still functioning on a lack of sleep and your worry about Sadie. At least we know now why they want her and they aren't going to harm her. If they were going to dump her somewhere, this would have been the perfect place. Apparently, they still need her and won't hurt her."

"Unless she can't do what they want her to, or she accomplishes what they want and then what are they going to do with her?" Annalise's tense question hung in the air.

Evan didn't have an answer to give her, but the possibilities of what might happen tortured him. He knew Jacob and his wife had no respect for human life. The man had already proven that. It was absolutely vital they find Sadie before Jacob and Gretchen decided the little girl was nothing more than a liability to them.

"I've got something," Davis said from the very back of the van. He pulled on something and then held up a license plate. "It was hidden in a slit in the carpeting."

"Good work, man." Evan took the license plate from the fellow agent. "Maybe this is the break we needed. Maybe finding out the registered owner of the van will give us more information."

Evan immediately got on the phone to Hendrick. He told the tech agent that the plate was a North Carolina plate, and he read out the numbers and letters.

"Arrange for the van to be taken into custody," he told his two men as he waited for a call back from Hendrick. He and Annalise got back into the rental car.

"We'll drive through someplace and grab some breakfast on our way back to the hotel." He shot her a quick glance. "Are you okay?"

She nodded. "I'm okay, but that message from Sadie really gutted me."

"At least it tells us she's still okay," he replied.

He swung through a drive-through, and they both ordered breakfast sandwiches. He'd just paid and received their order when Hendrick called back.

"The plates come back as belonging to an eight-seat black passenger van registered to Sandhurst School."

For just a moment Evan was speechless. He'd expected the name of a person, but this was definitely a shock. "I made a few calls and found out that the school owns three of these vans," Hendrick continued. "They are kept in a garage at a nearby vehicle rental lot, and I spoke to the owner who told me one of the vans went missing."

"There's no sign that the van has been hot-wired. Is the garage secure?" Evan asked.

"According to the owner, the vans are under lock and key. Only somebody with a key to the garage and the van could have driven one off. He hadn't even noticed that one of the vans was missing. He said he gave out four garage keys to the Sandhurst School."

"I'll make sure somebody goes to the garage and checks out the employees there," Evan said. "I know you've been busy doing other things for me, but I need the background reports on anyone who works at the school as soon as possible."

"I'll email what I already have for you and will keep digging."

"Thanks." Evan hung up.

"What does this mean?" Annalise asked.

"It's definitely an inside job," Evan said grimly.

"I can tell you that the garage and van keys were always kept on a hook in the school office for when a teacher wanted to plan a field trip."

Evan digested this information and tightened his hands on the steering wheel. Now he was not only determined to find Jacob and Gretchen and save Sadie, but also he wanted the rat that might have been responsible for setting all this in motion in the first place. He definitely wanted the insider.

Chapter Eight

They took their breakfast sandwiches to Evan's room and sat at the table to eat. She felt overwhelmed with everything that was happening.

If she looked deep inside herself, she knew she'd recognize that her vulnerable state wasn't only because of the heartrending message from Sadie, it was also because of Evan.

In the past three years she'd thought she'd moved on. She'd believed she'd gotten over him. But the truth of the matter was, she was surprised to realize she wasn't over him. He still owned a large piece of her heart and she didn't know what to do about it.

Right now they were both on a mission to save Sadie, and this wasn't the time or the place to explore those feelings. She didn't want to get in the way of Evan doing his job.

"I can't believe somebody at the school might be behind all this," she said as they ate. "That possibility absolutely blows my mind."

"Hopefully we'll know more when I get all the backgrounds from Hendrick." He looked at her for a long moment. "So, what happened with you and the college in Missouri? I thought teaching there was something you really wanted to do."

"You know when I was working in the public school system I was constantly battling for better and newer equipment for the students," she replied.

"I remember how frustrated you were by the constant lack of funding."

"When I got the offer from the college, it came with the assurance that my classes would be well-funded and the students would all have state-of-the-art equipment," she replied.

"So, that wasn't the case?"

She shook her head no. "As a teacher I had the absolute best equipment I could have asked for. It was a dream job as far as that was concerned."

"Then, why aren't you still working there?" he asked.

She frowned and stared down at her breakfast sandwich. "It didn't take me long to realize the students didn't care. They really didn't care about learning. Getting a degree from that particular college was a status symbol and nothing more. If the students didn't do well enough, then pressure was placed on the teachers to make sure they passed anyway. They were spoiled, rich kids with parents who indulged them far too much."

"I'm sure giving a student a grade they hadn't earned didn't sit well with you," he replied.

"Not even," she replied adamantly. "I hated it. I stayed there for almost two years but started putting my résumé out there again. Then last year I was offered a one-year contract with the school here. It really has been a dream position. Not only do I have whatever I need as an educator, but the students are like sponges who love to learn."

Once again tears blurred her vision as she thought of Sadie. She stared down, feeling foolish for her uncontrollable emotions. What was wrong with her? Maybe Evan was right; she was still functioning on too little sleep and her concerns for the little girl.

To her stunned surprise, he reached across the table and covered one of her hands with his. "We're going to find her, Annalise," he said with grim determination vibrating through his body and voice.

She turned her hand over and laced her fingers with his, surprised when he didn't immediately pull away. He had big, capable hands, and his larger hand nearly engulfed her smaller one. For a long moment they remained that way. She was the one to finally pull away.

Annalise released a deep sigh. "The two things that give me some bit of comfort is that Sadie is so smart and she's a survivor. Most of her life she endured being beaten and abused by her mother, and her father was never in her life. She was the one who helped me make the phone calls to you by serving as a lookout. She tried to protect me from Gretchen. She also interacted several times with Jacob, and I now wonder if she intentionally made herself the target to save the other girls who she knew weren't as strong as she was."

"Hopefully she's smart enough to know that we need help in locating her," he replied.

"She is," Annalise replied firmly. She had to believe that. She desperately needed to believe that when this was all over, Sadie would be saved.

As they finished eating, she continued to tell him more about working at Sandhurst School. "Regina Sandhurst has been a great boss." She frowned thoughtfully. "You know, now that I think about it, for the last couple of months Susan DeKalb has been worried about her finances, although I can't imagine how she or anyone else at the school would have come in contact with the likes of Jacob or Gretchen."

"Hopefully Hendrick can come up with some answers for us."

"My contract is up in December, and I'm not sure I'll sign another one."

He looked at her in surprise. "But it sounds like this was your dream job…great equipment and children who love to learn." He raised one of his dark eyebrows quizzically. "Would you not want to return because of what has happened?"

"No, something like this would never deter me from coming back to work. The real reason I'm probably going to return to Knoxville is because my father has been struggling with heart disease, and I think both my parents need me there."

It felt strange, sharing these things with him. It felt strange to be sharing anything with him. She'd never dreamed they'd ever see or talk to each other again.

"I'm assuming you're a rock star at TCD," she said. "I can't imagine you doing anything else."

He smiled. "You should know it's all in my blood, the pressure…the danger…and the desire to save people who find themselves in horrible situations. I'll work there as long as they'll have me."

"I'm sure they consider you a terrific asset," she replied.

He released a small, dry laugh. "You were always good at flattery."

"It's not empty flattery," she protested. "It's the truth. Look at the situation you just got us out of."

His smile faded and his eyes darkened. "Jacob and Gretchen got away with one of the hostages. Right now I consider this whole operation an epic fail."

"From what I've heard, the fail wasn't yours but rather that of local officials. You couldn't know that those officers would run and hide at the first gun shots outside the van window," she protested. She'd overheard just enough conversations to know what had happened.

"Yeah, but I should have made sure there were enough men in the back of the school to keep that van from leaving. I should have recognized the weakness, especially after working with Chief Cummings for any length of time."

"You can't control everything all the time, Evan. You're being way too hard on yourself," she said softly. "You did everything humanly possible. You need to cut yourself some slack."

He merely sighed and they fell into a silence. It wasn't a comfortable silence, rather it was charged with tension.

"Surely they've had enough time by now to find someplace to land," she said in frustration.

"We won't know that unless Hendrick comes up with something or Sadie gets access to a computer." He rubbed the back of his neck, a sign of his own frustration.

A knock fell on his door. He got up from the table. "Maybe that's one of my men with some new information."

He opened the door and over his shoulder Annalise saw a tall, brown-haired stranger. He offered Evan a tentative smile. "Are you Special Agent Duran?"

"I am," Evan replied.

"Uh... I have some news for you."

"And you are?" Evan asked.

The man shifted from one foot to the other, and his gaze shot from Evan to Annalise. "My name is Phil Sanders. I have some information about Jacob Noble. Uh...can I come in?"

"Why don't you just give me the information you have for me?" Evan replied.

He froze and Annalise gasped as Phil reached behind him and pulled a gun. There was a charged long minute of silence. Her heart raced, and every muscle in her body tensed with a fight or flight adrenaline rush.

"What do you want, Phil?" Evan asked calmly.

"The first thing I want is for you to toss your gun onto the bed, and if you make a wrong move, I'll kill you both."

Annalise gasped. Who was this man? What did he want? There were FBI and local authorities throughout the hotel. How had he managed to just walk up to Evan's door?

"That's not happening, so just tell me what you want," Evan replied, his voice still cool and calm.

The man looked frustrated. "I need you to get rid of your weapon."

"And I told you that isn't happening, so tell me what you want and why you're here or shoot me right now."

The man gestured with his gun for Evan to back up. He did so, and Phil stepped into the room and closed the door behind him. "I'm with the Brother-hood of Jacob, and I want you to call off the search for Jacob and Gretchen."

"And if I don't?"

Phil's blue eyes narrowed. "If you don't call off the search right now, then I'm going to kill you."

Annalise's heart banged hard against her ribs, making her half-breathless as she stared at the gun-man.

His hand shook as he held the weapon pointed at Evan's chest. "Stop the search for Jacob and Gretchen right now."

"Annalise, I want you to go into the bathroom and close and lock the door," Evan said.

"Don't move," Phil half shouted at her. He aimed the gun at her and then jerked it back to point at Evan.

"Go ahead, Annalise…" Evan said calmly.

"I'm not leaving you," she replied despite her fear. There was no way she was just going to run and hide in the bathroom and leave Evan to face this threat alone.

"Listen to me, Annalise," Evan said, his voice still calm and steady. "Focus on me. I need you to go to the bathroom and lock the door."

Annalise stood and held her position next to the table. "Don't move…don't move," Phil yelled at her. Sweat worked down the sides of his reddened face.

There was no way, no matter how many times Evan told her to go into the bathroom, she was leaving him. With both of them in the room, the man would be more apt to get distracted. If he did, then Evan would be able to take control of the situation.

"Phil, you need to calm down," Evan said.

"My job is to protect Jacob, so you need to stop the search for him right now. He's our leader, and he's doing good things for the world," Phil replied.

"Phil, I don't have the power to stop anything," Evan replied. "I couldn't stop this search right now if I wanted to. It's all out of my hands. So, you have two choices right now—either kill me or put the gun down and let's talk."

"You have the power," Phil screamed. "Stop the damned search. Jacob has to be protected."

Annalise took two steps forward and then paused. Her fear was all-consuming. Phil looked half-deranged as he faced them. How had this happened? How had the man even found out where they were staying?

"Nobody can protect Jacob anymore," Evan said softly. "Jacob and Gretchen have made some really bad mistakes. Now why don't you put your gun down, and you can tell me about the good work the members of the Brotherhood do."

The gun in Phil's hand began to shake as he looked from Evan to Annalise. She took another step forward, and Phil's eyes widened in panic.

"Look at me, Phil," Evan said. "Give me your gun, Phil." Evan's voice was almost hypnotic, and she knew his use of Phil's name was to let the man know Evan really saw him and wanted to interact with him.

It was one of his strengths as a hostage negotiator...making people feel comfortable...making people want to talk to him. While it hadn't worked with Jacob, it appeared to be working on Phil, who looked far less sure of himself than he had when he'd initially confronted Evan.

"Come on, Phil. I know you're a good man who wants to do the right thing," Evan continued. "I'm sure you didn't know what Jacob and the rest of the men were planning. People died, Phil. When they went into the school they killed good people who were just going about their daily lives and doing their jobs."

"None of us back at the compound had any idea they were going to bust into a school," Phil admitted.

Evan took a step toward him and then reached out and took hold of the barrel of the gun. Phil began to weep as he finally relinquished the weapon.

Evan led him to the edge of the bed and grabbed his cell phone. As Phil continued to cry, Evan made a quick call to Davis. Annalise sank back down at the table as a sigh of relief escaped her.

"You don't understand," Phil said as Evan hung up. "Jacob and Gretchen control everything. They tell us all what to do and we do it. They've always told us how to live our daily lives. We...we...none of us know how to survive without them."

"Phil, I'm sure you're all smart and resourceful people. Everyone will have to find a way without them," Evan replied smoothly.

"I don't even know why he went to that school in the first place." Phil swiped at his tears. "He didn't tell all of us exactly what his plans were. If I hadn't seen it on the news, I wouldn't have known they were all in that school."

"It's going to be okay, Phil. You're going to be just fine," Evan replied with assurance.

Annalise's admiration for Evan soared off the charts. Moments before, Phil had held Evan at gunpoint and threatened to kill him. Now he was talking to that same man in a calm and respectful and compassionate way.

Phil explained to Evan he'd hidden out in a storage closet until the halls were quiet, and then he'd come to the room. He'd also told them there were others at the compound who knew not only the hotel where FBI agents were staying, but also Evan's room number.

She remained silent at the table and listened to the two men talk. Finally Davis appeared at the door with Nick, and the two men left with Phil in their custody.

Evan walked back to the bed, sank down and then looked at her. "Are you okay?"

"My heart is still beating faster than it should, but I'm fine."

"Why didn't you do what I asked of you? You should have gone into the bathroom."

"I thought it was better for me not to remove myself from the room," she countered. "I figured two of us would be more of a distraction to him. As it is, it all worked out okay."

"Until we neutralize this situation, I need you to listen to me." He offered her a faint smile. "You know how I like to control my crime scenes."

"I do. Would it be possible for you to work this scene from my house instead of this hotel? I'd love to go home. I have all the office equipment we would need… We can set up a command center in my living room. I also have three bedrooms. That way we wouldn't be spending all our time in these hotel rooms. Think about it, Evan. My place is only five minutes from here."

He frowned thoughtfully. "I don't like the fact that members of this group now know where we are staying. I don't want to have to use additional resources to make sure this doesn't happen again."

"What I worry about is that the next person from the compound who shows up here will shoot first instead of talk. They might all blame you for everything because you were the main man on the scene," she replied.

He frowned, obviously thinking it through.

"Evan, let's just pack up and go. It makes sense." She wasn't sure why, but she suddenly realized she needed to be back in her own home.

She wanted her familiar things surrounding her. It felt like it had been months and months since she'd been home. Right now her emotions were all over the place. She was frightened for Sadie, and her feelings where Evan was concerned were so unsettled.

The confines of a hotel room felt far too intimate, and at least if they were working from her house she could feel like she had a little distance from Evan... distance that might help her sort out her crazy emotions about him.

This wasn't over yet. She had no idea how long it might be before it was over. Hopefully it would end with Sadie's rescue and clarity for her where Evan was concerned.

She got up from the table and sank down on the bed next to him. "I just want you to know that I was impressed with how you handled Phil."

"I had a pretty good idea that he wasn't going to shoot anyone," he replied.

"But how did you know that?"

He smiled at her. "Annalise, I'm trained to know that. I look for certain tells. More than anything I could see his fear. He held the weapon without any real confidence, and he was far too emotional. Besides, he didn't have a killer's eyes."

She returned his smile. "I always told you that you're the best hostage negotiator in the whole wide world."

His dark gaze softened. "And I always said that you were the most beautiful woman in the whole wide world."

He was too close to her. Her breath suddenly felt a bit labored as the moment between them lingered. His thigh pressed against hers, his warm body intimately near, and as the residual fear she'd felt earlier completely drained away from her another emotion surfaced.

Desire.

It rocked through her and flushed her entire body with a sweet warmth. He felt it, too. She saw it in the sudden burn of his eyes as he gazed at her.

She leaned closer and parted her lips in invitation. Her heart stuttered to a near halt as she waited to see what he was going to do. And then his lips were on hers. At first it was a hesitant, tender kiss, but then it became more insistent, far more demanding as his tongue swirled with hers.

His hands tangled in her hair, and she turned to

grip his shoulders. Oh, she'd missed this…she'd so missed him. His mouth felt so familiar and yet at the same time so exciting and new to her.

The kiss spoke to a place deep inside her that had been dormant since the day they had parted ways, a place that now felt alive and as necessary as the very air she breathed.

"Annalise," he moaned as his mouth left hers and found the spot just behind her ear that often drove her wild with desire. He then blazed a trail of nipping kisses down the side of her neck.

How on earth had she ever walked away from this man? His simplest touch electrified her, and his kisses made her feel more alive than any man she had ever dated before or would probably ever date in the future.

Slowly his hands untangled from her hair and moved down her back. He pressed her tightly against him as once again his mouth found hers for another soul-stirring kiss.

She wanted him. She leaned back, pulling him with her so they both were lying on the bed. She could feel his heart beating rapidly against her own, letting her know he wanted her as much as she wanted him.

One of his hands began to caress her stomach, each stroke bringing him closer and closer to her breasts. She wanted his touch. Oh, dear heaven, she wanted them both naked and moving together beneath the sheets.

"Evan." She breathed his name as his mouth once

again left hers. As he kissed down the side of her cheek, his beard created an additional pleasant sensation.

Finally his hand covered one of her breasts. Even though she wore a T-shirt and a bra, her nipples hardened as if eager for a more intimate touch.

She pushed against him and raised up just enough to pull the T-shirt over her head and toss it to the other side of the bed.

He unbuttoned and took his shirt off as well, and once again they came together. Her skin remembered the warmth and pleasure of his. As they kissed, their tongues once again swirled together in a wild dance of half-breathless passion. His fingers moved to her bra hooks…

At that moment a knock fell on the door.

Evan jumped up, half-dazed with his desire for her. He grabbed his shirt and quickly buttoned it while Annalise grabbed her T-shirt and ran for the bathroom.

He drew in a deep breath, grabbed his gun from the nightstand and then opened the door to see Davis. "I just wanted to let you know that Phil is now a guest in Chief Cummings's jail."

"Thanks, man. I'm now wondering if all the members of that group are as rabid as Phil."

"Whatever they call themselves, they are definitely a cult," Davis replied. "According to Phil, a bunch of them are planning to set up a protest of some kind later this evening outside the hotel. I have a feeling it's going to be a circus."

That made up Evan's mind. The last thing he wanted was to try to stay focused and concentrate while a bunch of crazy cult members set up camp outside the hotel. Davis nodded to Annalise as she returned to the room.

"Annalise has offered the use of her house to me…and I'm going to take her up on it."

He had to admit that what had happened just before Davis had knocked on the door had shocked him. His desire for her had caught him off guard, and he didn't want that to happen again. Surely a house would be less intimate than the hotel rooms, and it really didn't matter where he did his work.

"My place is only minutes from here," she said to Davis.

"Sounds like a perfect way to avoid the circus that might go on here," Davis replied. "It's going to be difficult to completely secure the hotel now, and that's going to take manpower. Instead of being out looking for the fugitives, a bunch of officers will now have to be here. When are you planning on making the move?"

"As soon as we can," Evan said. He could see no downside to moving to her house.

"Then I'll get out of here," Davis replied.

"I'll text you and the others as soon as we're settled at Annalise's place," Evan said.

Once Davis was gone, he turned to Annalise. "You need to get packed up."

She stared at him for a long moment. "Shouldn't we talk about what just happened between us?"

"There isn't much to talk about," he replied. "Adrenaline was running high. We'd just been through a tense situation with Phil, and what happened between us was a mistake and we need to make sure it doesn't happen again. I've got a missing child and two dangerous fugitives on the run, and I need to be completely focused on that."

"And I want you to be completely focused on getting Sadie back, but I will tell you it didn't feel like a mistake to me. It felt wonderful, and now I'll go pack up my things."

When she left the room, Evan drew in a deep breath. Yes, it had been wonderful to have her in his arms again, but he wasn't here to explore a relationship with her. He had a job to do.

Thirty minutes later they were in the rental car and heading to Annalise's home. The ride was silent other than her giving him directions. He was grateful for the silence and he used it to recenter himself.

Annalise's rental ranch house was located in a quiet neighborhood with lots of mature trees. The first thing he did when they arrived was a quick walk around the house to orient himself to his new surroundings. Then she guided him into a pleasant living room decorated in browns and golds.

"You can use this bedroom," she said as she showed him to one of the guest rooms.

He scarcely noticed the bedroom, instead intent on getting his work area ready. The dining room table was large, and on a desk nearby was her computer with a large monitor. He set up his computer on the table and immediately checked in with Davis, Nick and Daniel back at the hotel.

While he was talking to his men, Annalise powered up her computer at the desk. He checked his watch, shocked to realize it was only a little after two in the afternoon.

He definitely wanted to have Sadie back before nightfall and right now he racked his brain to see what else he could do to make that happen.

HENDRICK AWOKE WITH a start. He sat up, raised a hand, raced it through his hair and tried to shrug off the last of his sleep.

When Director Pembrook had insisted he needed to get some rest, he'd finally gone to a break room where there were several cots for the agents to use. He'd fallen asleep almost as soon as his head had touched the pillow.

He checked his watch, thankful that he'd only been out for about two hours. What was going on with the case? What had he missed while he'd slept? He hoped it was all over, that Sadie had been found and Jacob and his creepy wife were behind bars.

He got up and headed to the locker room for a quick shower. Once the shower was done, he changed into a clean pair of jeans and a T-shirt from his locker.

Immediately after that he headed to the nearest coffee machine. He filled up a disposable cup with the dark brew and then hurried to the tech office where Agent Curt Corkland was seated in front of the computers.

"Hey, man, anything happening?" he asked.

"You weren't down for very long," Curt said. "I didn't expect you back so soon."

"I feel pretty refreshed. I've never required too much sleep. So, tell me what's going on?"

"I've just been working on gathering the backgrounds on some of the school faculty members. So far nothing is bringing up any red flags. There are still a few to check out."

Hendrick frowned. "Evan seems certain that Jacob and Gretchen had inside information when they entered the school, and the van belonging to the school seems to confirm that. I just want to catch that rat."

"Well, there are a few more people I haven't gotten to yet. Maybe you'll find your rat among them," Curt said.

"Heard anything from Evan?"

Curt shook his head. "No, nothing from anyone."

Hendrick took a drink of his coffee and motioned Curt up and out of the seat. "I'm good now. Thanks for manning the post."

"No prob," Curt replied. He showed him the list of faculty and staff that he'd managed to get through so far, and then he left the room.

Hendrick settled in his chair and began the background search on the next person on the list. He'd been dividing the background checks, not only checking out the staff at the school, but also the members from the Brotherhood of Jacob. He was trying to discover if any of them had any property anywhere, any place where Jacob and Gretchen might be able to go into hiding.

He clicked over to the page where Annalise hoped Sadie would make contact. So far…nothing. He took another drink of his coffee and fought against a level of frustration he'd rarely felt since leaving the cult behind.

Before going down for his brief rest, he'd also been in touch with the men at the compound who were sending him the tag numbers of the cars coming and going. Hendrick had been pulling up DMV records to identify the owners.

His biggest fear was that the vehicle Jacob was now using was one that had left the compound before the police presence there had been established. It was also possible somebody connected to the school had provided Jacob with another ride. Who in the hell was the insider who had helped organize the evil that had taken place at the school?

Another night would soon approach, and the more time that passed the less the odds were of finding Sadie alive. God, he wanted to help rescue this kid. He needed her to be okay.

Despite the fact he knew it wasn't true, he felt somehow if they didn't manage to save little Sadie, then it would mean he'd never really escaped the bonds of the cult that had nearly destroyed him.

Chapter Nine

It felt odd being in her house, among her things. She made them sandwiches, and then they settled side by side at the table to eat.

After two years with Annalise, Evan knew what was important to her and what was not. Almost three years had passed since they'd been in each other's lives, but he didn't really want to know anything more about her than he already knew. He didn't want to open any doors that had already been closed.

Yeah, it had been great to hold her, to kiss her once again, but he told himself their brief intimacy had been the result of adrenaline from facing Phil and the frustration from where things stood in the investigation. He told himself it had really meant nothing to him.

They ate quickly and without much conversation. When they finished, she settled at her computer at the desk and he got on the phone to check the status of all the arms of the investigation.

When Annalise's doorbell rang, he jumped up from the table and pulled his gun. He wasn't about to get caught unaware again. Annalise got up as well and followed him to answer the door.

He opened it to see Rowan. "Hey, Rowan," he said, and immediately holstered his gun and gestured her into the house. "What's going on?"

"I just wanted to check in with you before I head back to headquarters," she said.

"You're leaving me here all alone with that waste of a police chief?" he asked.

Rowan grinned. "Afraid so. Director Pembrook called me back to Knoxville. Besides, your interaction with Chief Cummings should be fairly minimal at this point. I have confidence that you can handle it."

"Well, that makes one of us," he replied dryly.

"Evan, just don't kill him. It would make a mess of paperwork for everyone," she replied with a small laugh.

"Rowan, I want to thank you for the personal items you got for me," Annalise said. "I really appreciate it."

"No problem," she replied.

Annalise reached into her pocket and pulled out the cell phone. "I'm assuming you need this back now."

"That's okay. Keep it until Evan leaves and then you can give it to him," Rowan said, and then gazed back at Evan. "It's actually good that you two relocated here. When I left the hotel, there were about a dozen people from the compound already there for some sort of protest against law enforcement and the FBI. They have big signs declaring police abuse and all kinds of crazy things."

Evan grimaced. "Sounds like the police are going to have their hands full there." He smiled once again at Rowan. "Thanks, Rowan, as always, for everything you did to support the team."

Her eyes twinkled with humor. "I have to admit there were a couple of times when I wanted to hogtie Chief Cummings and toss him in a barn far, far away."

Evan laughed. "There were definitely times I would have helped you with that."

"Okay, then I'm off," Rowan replied. She smiled at Annalise and then looked back at him. "I know you, Evan, and I hope you aren't beating yourself up about how this has turned out so far. I know you'll get these SOBs."

"Thanks, Rowan."

Evan walked her to the door, and once she was gone he had just sat back at the dining room table when Annalise's computer dinged with a notification. Hope speared through him as he jumped up and Annalise raced across the room to the desk. A nonsensical sentence had appeared on the special page.

He couldn't help the excitement that roared through him. Was this it? Was this finally what they had been waiting for? A note from Sadie letting them know where she was being held?

"It's not from Sadie," she said flatly. "It's from Emily."

Evan's heart plummeted. "What does it say?"

"It says, 'Sadie, I know you're missing. Where are you? We're all worried about you.'"

"You need to get on there and ask the other girls not to post anything to the page until Sadie is found," he said.

Annalise nodded and sat at the desk. She typed what looked like an equally nonsensical message and then hit enter. "Now, let's hope the next person who posts here is Sadie," he said.

He sank back down in his chair and released a deep sigh. "When I heard that notification go off, I was sure it was her."

"I feel like this is some form of terrible torture… waiting for her to make contact with us," she said. "What happens if she doesn't? What happens if I'm wrong about this or she doesn't get any opportunity to get on the page?"

"Right now Jacob and Gretchen are on every wanted list in the nation. Law enforcement agencies all over the area will be on the lookout for them. Sooner or later they will make a mistake, and we'll find them."

She held his gaze for a long moment and then with a nod she went into the kitchen. With disappointment weighing heavily in his heart, his thoughts turned to the woman who had just disappeared from the room.

What was wrong with him? He could face an armed gunman locked in a building with his wife and kids as hostages without breaking a sweat, but being in the same space as Annalise was…difficult.

He was haunted by the ghosts of their past, tormented by how badly he'd misread her at the time and the love he'd thought they had shared.

He had to stay focused on the fact that she was an important piece of the puzzle of a missing child and nothing more. However, it did bother him that after almost three years apart he still had such strong emotions where she was concerned. It had been far easier to ignore these emotions when he had been in Knoxville and believed she had been in Missouri.

Now he was in her home and still desperate to find a little girl who was missing and in extreme danger. He drew a weary sigh and recognized his thoughts were flying all over the place. It was probably the lack of sleep. All he needed was to fuel himself with some caffeine.

When Annalise came back into the room, he asked her about coffee. "I'll get you a cup," she offered. "But while you're here, I want you to feel free to use whatever you need in the kitchen or anywhere else."

"Thanks," he replied.

Minutes later they were back at their computers. He was grateful when Hendrick called. "Hey, I think I might have a couple of live ones for you. In doing background on the school staff, some red flags have come up."

"Who?" Evan sat up straighter in his chair, all thoughts of weariness gone.

"An English teacher named Susan DeKalb and a janitor named Earl Winslow."

"Teacher first," Evan said. He was aware of Annalise listening intently to the conversation.

"Susan DeKalb is sixty-three years old and according to the financials I have, she's completely broke. Six months ago she pulled out her retirement funds and put her life savings into a restaurant her son owned, and it's now gone belly-up. She's looking at retirement with only a very small pension and a social security check."

Evan frowned thoughtfully. "So, it's possible she's helping Jacob out for a financial benefit."

"That was my thought. Unfortunately, I haven't found a connection between her and the Brotherhood of Jacob and any of its members. I'm still digging into that aspect."

"And what about this Earl Winslow?" Evan asked.

"Also financially struggling. He was hired less than a year ago as a janitor after not having worked for several years. Also a search of his name pulled up a three-month-old newspaper picture of him attending a sort of open house at the Brotherhood of Jacob compound."

Evan's blood quickened. Had one of these people sold out their coworkers and the students for a deal with the devil? There was no question he believed the motive for all of this was money.

He got off the phone with Hendrick and immediately called Chief Cummings and arranged for the police to pick up the teacher and the janitor for interviews inside the police station.

"I'm heading out," he said to Annalise. "I'm not sure when I'll be back here. Text me if Sadie writes you?"

"Of course," Annalise replied. "I'll keep you posted."

"Make sure you lock the door after me and don't open it to anyone you don't know," he said.

"Trust me, I won't," she replied. Annalise reached into a vase that stood on a stand next to her front door. "Here's the spare key."

"Thanks." He quickly attached it to his key ring.

"I hope you find some information that will help."

"So do I."

Maybe they didn't need Sadie to make contact to break the case wide open, he thought as he flew out of Annalise's front door. Maybe, just maybe the rat was at this very moment being rounded up by the local police.

THE MOMENT EVAN was gone, Annalise sat down at her computer with a thoughtful frown. Susan and Earl? Was it really possible that one of them was working with Jacob and Gretchen? Was it really possible that one of those trusted people had put fellow teachers and students at risk for their very lives? Had one of them participated in a scheme that had seen three people killed?

It was so hard to believe that anyone she knew could be a part of this, and yet somebody in the day-to-day life at the school had to be involved. Both Susan and Earl would have access to the van and garage keys that hung in the office. Both would know that on a Tuesday afternoon Annalise would be in the school building after hours with her smartest students.

Although she knew nothing about Earl's finances, she did know that Susan had been terribly concerned about her future after her son's restaurant had failed. Susan had divorced years ago and so had no one to share the financial burdens. She also knew that Sadie was terrific on the computer.

If one of them was behind this, she knew without a doubt Evan would ferret out the guilty and surely that person would know where Jacob and Gretchen had taken Sadie.

In the meantime she tapped her fingernails on her mouse pad. "Come on, Sadie. Talk to me."

Tears blurred her vision. Had she not heard anything from the little girl yet because it was already too late? Was it possible that Sadie had been unable to do what they'd asked and she was now dead?

There were plenty of heavily wooded and mountainous areas where a dumped body might take years to find, if ever. "Please, please, don't let Sadie be lost forever," she whispered aloud.

Annalise didn't know how long she sat watching the page before a deep weariness overtook her. She got up and stepped out on her back porch where woods encroached on her backyard.

She stared for several long minutes at the tall trees and brush, which normally brought her a sense of peace. This evening they only brought her more dreadful thoughts about Sadie.

She stood out there for only a few minutes and then returned to the house. After grabbing an afghan from the hall closet, she went to sit on the sofa and pulled the blanket around her shoulders. Her thoughts of Sadie and deep, dark woods had created a chill inside her.

Annalise glanced over at the computer and a new weariness struck her. She had her notifications turned up loud enough that if she did doze off the sound would awaken her.

With all the stress of the crime and worry about Sadie, she'd scarcely had time to process her feelings toward Evan. There was no doubt there was still something there. She didn't want to distract him from doing his job, but she hoped when this was all over, when the bad guys were behind bars and Sadie was back safely, she could have a real discussion with Evan about them.

When she'd been in the school, he'd said he'd had regrets, but the conversation had been interrupted before he could explain. She wanted to hear about his regrets, and she wanted to tell him about her own.

Yes, she hoped to have a conversation with him about what had gone wrong and the possibility of a second chance to get it right.

But first and more important, they had to find Sadie.

CHIEF CUMMINGS MET Evan at the front door of the police station. "I've got Susan DeKalb in a conference room, and an officer is on his way with Earl Winslow in tow. You want to tell me what's going on?"

"A few red flags have come up in their backgrounds that warrant a closer look at them," Evan replied.

"How do you want to approach this? Good cop, bad cop?" Cummings puffed out his chest. "I can definitely work the bad cop role."

"I don't think that will be necessary." Evan couldn't think of anything more ridiculous that Walter playing the role of bad cop. "I can handle this," Evan replied.

The chief frowned. "I will be sitting in on these interviews. I need to know what's going on."

"Of course." Evan just hoped Chief Cummings didn't do anything to interfere with the interviews. All Evan wanted to do was ferret out the guilty.

As he followed the chief down a short hallway to the conference room, he carried with him transcripts of the initial interviews that had been conducted on scene with the two employees by Nick and what Hendrick had discovered about the pair.

Evan hadn't met Earl yet, but he remembered Susan DeKalb and how desperate she had been for answers when she'd talked to him. Now he was the one needing answers.

She stood when the two men entered the room.

"What's happening? Why am I here?" she asked with obvious nervousness.

"Please, sit down," Evan said. "I just have a few things we want to clear up with you." He offered her a smile, hoping to put her at ease. People who were more comfortable and at ease often talked too much.

"Would you like something to drink before we get started?" Evan asked as she sank back down at the table. "Maybe some coffee or a soda?"

"No, thank you. I just want to understand why I'm here," she replied.

Evan sat across from her, and Chief Cummings sat next to him. "You should know that we've been checking out the backgrounds of everyone who works at the school. We believe the hostage takers had somebody on the inside who gave them information, and in checking into your background, a few things came to our attention."

Susan's eyes widened and her lower lip trembled. "You believe somebody at the school was working with those horrible people? That I was...that I am somehow involved?"

She looked at Chief Cummings and then back at Evan as her eyes filled with tears. "I would never... I could never be a part of something like this. What would make you believe that I might be?"

"We believe the person involved in this was hoping for a big monetary gain," Evan said.

"Is this about me losing money in my son's restaurant?" she asked. "I understood the risk when I gave it to him, but that doesn't mean I would invite monsters into the school."

As they continued to talk, Evan watched her body language carefully, seeking tells of deception. By the time the interview was over, Evan was certain Susan wasn't the rat he sought. For what it was worth, Chief Cummings agreed with his assessment.

Earl Winslow was a thin, wiry fifty-two-year-old with an attitude. When led into the room, he slammed himself into the chair and gazed defiantly at the two law officers.

"I really got better things to do than hanging out here," he said. "So, what's up?"

"Be nice, Earl. Special Agent Duran has some questions for you," Chief Cummings said.

"I just had some follow-up questions concerning what happened at the school," Evan said. "I understand you haven't been working there that long."

"About six months or so," Earl replied.

"And your last job before being hired on at the school?" Evan asked.

Earl frowned. "I worked as a house painter."

"But according to my records that was three years ago. I imagine financially things have been pretty tight for you," Evan said. Once again he watched Earl carefully, seeking any sign of deception.

"I'm not going to lie to you. There's been some lean times, but I lead a fairly simple life. What does my financial state have to do with what happened at the school?" Earl changed positions in the chair

and looked at Chief Cummings. "Come on, Walter…
what the hell is this really about?"

"It's about your involvement with what happened
at the school," the chief replied.

"My involvement?" Earl sat up straighter in the
chair. "What in the hell are you talking about? I
didn't have any involvement with anything."

"How long have you known Jacob Noble?" Evan
asked.

Earl's eyes narrowed almost imperceptibly. His
chin shot up just a notch. "Jacob Noble? I don't know
the man at all."

"I have evidence to the contrary," Evan replied.

Earl stared at him for a long moment and then
nodded and averted his gaze to someplace over Evan's head. "Okay, I met him a couple of months ago
when they held a rally. I went to the compound to
see what it was about. I'd heard it was kind of like
a commune where they grew their own vegetables
and all lived together in peace. I was only there for
about fifteen minutes before I realized Jacob and
his wife were crazy."

"Is that the only contact you had with the Brotherhood of Jacob?" Evan asked.

"Definitely. I left there and that was the end of it."

"I'm sure you have had a chance to interact with
the students at the school." Evan thumbed through
his notes, as if seeking more information.

"Not really. I see them in the hallways and I nod
and smile, but that's about it," Earl replied, looking
more and more uncomfortable with the conversa-

tion. "Look, I had nothing to do with this. I'd never do anything that might hurt those kids."

"Do you have a cell phone?" Evan already knew the answer because he could see the device in Earl's breast pocket.

"Yeah…why?" Earl's dark eyes narrowed once again.

"Do you mind if I see it?" Evan asked.

"Yeah, I do mind. I think you need a warrant for that." He got up from the table. "Walter, you've known me for years. You should know I'd never be involved with anything like the slaughter that happened in the school. Sure, I met Jacob one time because I was curious about life in the compound. I never talked to him again. I never planned anything with him. You got the wrong guy and now I'm done here. If you aren't going to arrest me, then you'd better arrange a ride for me to go home."

"He's our man," Chief Cummings said the moment Earl left the small conference room. "I feel it in my gut, and my gut is never wrong. He's definitely guilty. Why didn't you arrest him?"

"Because we don't have the evidence to arrest him right now," Evan replied curtly. "Put a couple of tails on him. If he is our man, maybe he'll lead us to where Jacob and Gretchen are holed up."

"Consider it done. But I've got to tell you, I definitely feel like we got our inside man." Chief Cummings appeared positively jubilant. Evan wasn't so sure.

He'd have Hendrick work with the cell phone

company to get Earl's texts and a log of incoming and outgoing calls. Of course it was always possible that if Earl really was involved, he might be smart enough to own a burner phone that would be less easy to trace.

"Earl has always been a strange duck. He's never married and is a loner. He lives in a little house his parents owned before they died, but I heard he owes some back taxes on it and is about to lose it. I'm telling you, he's our man, Agent Duran."

Evan got up from the table. "Put the tails on him and let me know if anything breaks. I'll touch base with you sometime tomorrow."

Minutes later Evan stepped outside the police station, surprised that night was approaching and with it a deep exhaustion he couldn't deny. It had been a wild day, from Phil accosting them with a gun, the move to Annalise's home and finally a potential piece of the puzzle.

But, he was functioning on two hours of sleep, and at the moment he was so exhausted his thoughts were muddled. As he drove back to Annalise's place, he thought about the interview with Earl. While the fact that the man had met Jacob a month before was suspicious, it was also possible it was one of those odd coincidences that life sometimes sets up. The last thing he wanted was a rush to justice that might see an innocent man behind bars and the guilty still free.

He let himself in with the spare key Annalise had given him. He walked into the living room to find her talking about code on a video chat with Hendrick. For a moment he merely stood there and listened.

She was brilliant. That was part of what had drawn him to her in the first place. The fact that she could hold her own with one of the FBI's top techs was remarkable.

She must have sensed his presence for she looked over her shoulder and smiled, then turned back to the computer. "Evan just walked in," she said to the tech agent.

"Evan. Anything new come out of the interviews?" Hendrick asked.

Evan stepped into camera view and caught Hendrick up with what he'd learned from Susan and Earl. "Chief Cummings is convinced Earl is our man, and he was ready to make an arrest immediately."

"And what did you think?" Hendrick asked.

"I think we need a lot more information than what I have," Evan replied. The two men talked for another few minutes, and when they finished Hendrick said goodbye to Annalise and then he disconnected.

"Are you okay?" Annalise asked.

Evan sank down on the edge of the sofa. "To be honest, I'm completely exhausted. I assume you still haven't heard from Sadie?"

"You assume right, and you probably need to crash for the night. I have to confess I napped almost the whole time you were gone. So I'm good to man the computers while you get some sleep."

He rubbed the back of his neck. "Maybe I'll just stretch out right here on the sofa for an hour."

"Are you sure you don't want to go back to a bed?" she asked.

"Nah, I'll be fine right here."

"I'll go get you a pillow to make you more comfortable," she replied.

As she left the room, Evan's thoughts went wild. The whole plot had been for Jacob to grab Sadie to break into the banking system. Sooner or later if their plan was still the same, Sadie would be put in front of a computer. Whether or not she would get an opportunity to type on Annalise's page was another thing altogether. If the little girl was as smart as Annalise said she was, then one way or another she'd figure out a way to make contact.

He seriously doubted that Sadie would make any contact tonight. If they'd spent the day still on the run, then Jacob and Gretchen had to be exhausted, as well.

They would need to crash someplace and sleep. Or, it was possible they'd already landed somewhere and had spent the day catching up on sleep. And then there was Earl Winslow. Was he the insider who had told them which girl to grab and had provided the keys to the van and garage so they could drive in a Sandhurst vehicle? If the van was found, would it only lead the authorities around in circles?

God, his thoughts were going around and around

in his head and making him half-crazy. Had he over-looked anything? Was everything possible being done to find the fugitives?

He wished he didn't need sleep. There were times he hated that he was only human and required rest. But he knew by the way his mind was working he definitely needed a little sleep.

Annalise returned with a pillow. "Are you sure you don't want to go back in the bedroom?" she asked one more time.

"I'll be fine here…unless I'll bother you." He took the pillow from her.

"You won't bother me. I'll just sit tight here at my desk and watch for any sign from Sadie." She turned off the overhead light, leaving the room il-luminated only by a desk lamp.

Evan stretched out with a deep sigh. He didn't want to think about the fact that he was oddly com-forted that Annalise was so nearby, that they were both fighting side by side to save a little girl.

He definitely didn't want to think about what would happen to him…to her…to them if in the end, Sadie wasn't saved.

Chapter Ten

Annalise jerked awake, surprised to realize she'd nodded off in her desk chair. The clock said it was just after midnight, and with a quick glance around she immediately knew what had awakened her.

Evan was having one of his nightmares. He'd had them occasionally when they had been together, although he'd never shared with her what they were about. He tossed and turned, his features twisted as he breathed rapidly...harshly.

Her first instinct was to wake him, to get him out of wherever he was in his sleep landscape. But she paused and hoped the nightmare would pass and he'd continue to get some more much-needed sleep.

His thrashing grew more intense, and Annalise half rose from her chair, afraid that he would end up falling off the sofa. "Maria!" The name exploded out of him and he bolted upright. He swiped his hands down the sides of his face and released a deep breath.

"Evan, are you okay?" Annalise asked softly. "You were having one of your nightmares."

"Yeah, I'm fine." He swung his legs off the sofa and sat up. "What time is it?"

"Just a little after midnight. Evan, who is Maria?"

She was sorry she'd asked him the question the minute it left her mouth and she saw his reaction. His face paled as he sat up straighter. "How do you know anything about Maria?" he asked.

"I don't know anything about her. You just called out her name and now I'm curious."

He held her gaze for a long moment and reached a hand up to rub the back of his neck. He broke eye contact with her and stared down at the coffee table, but before he did so she saw what appeared to be stark grief sweep over his features.

He released an audible sigh. "Maria is...was my younger sister."

She looked at him in stunned surprise. She'd met his mother on a trip they had taken to New York, but in the two years they had dated Evan had never mentioned he had a sister. She'd always thought it was just he and his mother.

"You never told me about her," she said.

"There's not much to tell. I don't know if she's dead or alive. She disappeared when she was five years old."

Annalise gasped. "Disappeared? What do you mean? What exactly happened?" She got up from the desk and sank down next to him on the sofa.

He immediately stood and began to pace back and forth in front of her. The grief she'd seen momentarily before now captured his features once again, along with something else…some emotion she couldn't quite identify. "Tell me, Evan," she said softly.

"It was an early evening on a Tuesday. My mom had worked all day cleaning a couple of really nasty apartments for our landlord. She was hot and exhausted by the time she got home. All she asked was that I take Maria outside for about an hour or so to let her take a quick shower and catch a nap."

Annalise could feel the tension that wafted from him as he continued to pace back and forth. "How old were you at the time?" she asked.

"Eight. I was eight years old and she was five. I loved my little sister so much." His voice cracked slightly. "Even though I was older than her, she was like my best friend. She could be a pest, but I loved her anyway."

He paused and drew in a deep breath, then released it on a shuddering sigh. "So, I took Maria outside. I remember it was a hot summer evening. Maria had a piece of sidewalk chalk. It was purple, and she sat on the stoop and was drawing pictures of me while I made goofy poses."

His dark eyes grew distant, and for just a moment a faint smile curved his lips. "I'd act goofy all the time just to make her laugh. She had such a wonderful giggle."

The smile faded and his eyes grew darker. "We were outside for probably half an hour or so when some of my buddies came walking up the sidewalk.

I went to talk to them, and at the same time Maria chased a butterfly into the alley."

He stopped pacing and stood in front of her. A deep, raw pain emanated from his eyes. "I greeted my friends and then I went to get Maria. I went into the alley…and…and a man was there. He had Maria and he had a big knife."

He drew in another deep breath. "I wanted to save her. I needed to save her, but I didn't. The man ran away with her and…and we never saw her again."

She couldn't stand to see his anguish any longer. She got up from the sofa and took his hand in hers, then pulled him down to sit next to her.

She held his hand tightly. "My God, Evan. Why have you never told me about this before?"

His dark gaze held hers and then looked away. "Why would I have told you that I was responsible for the kidnapping of my little sister? Why would I share that with the woman I loved?"

"Evan, you were just a little boy. You should have never had that kind of responsibility on you in the first place."

"But I took on the responsibility and I screwed up," he replied. "I should have never stopped to say hi to my friends. I should have never taken my attention off her. I definitely should have never allowed Maria to chase a damned butterfly into the alley."

"What did the police do?" She continued to hold his hand as she watched the emotions playing on his handsome features. Loss…grief…guilt, they were all there.

He released a deep bitter laugh. "They found nothing in the alley, no evidence, no leads to find her. All they had was my description of the man, and all I could tell them was that the kidnapper was a tall, white man with shaggy brown hair."

"So, they never caught him?"

He shook his head. "Even though my mother called the police station every day, if felt like nobody really cared. My mother thought they didn't do a real investigation because we were poor and Latino."

"I certainly hope that wasn't true," she replied, appalled by the mere notion.

"The idea that it might be was what drove me into the law enforcement field." He released a deep sigh. "I've never stopped looking for Maria. I check the internet to this day hoping to find her out there somewhere."

"I'm sorry, Evan. I'm so sorry for your loss," she replied softly. She knew her words were inadequate, but she meant them to the depths of her soul.

She couldn't believe he'd had something so catastrophic happen to him when he'd been so young and impressionable, and during the two years they'd dated he'd never told her anything about it.

She gazed at him and he looked at her at the same time. His face was so near to hers. His lips were achingly close. He leaned forward and her breath caught in her throat as she anticipated a kiss.

His lips almost grazed hers, and then he jerked

upright and off the sofa. "I need to check in with some people."

The night hours passed slowly. Evan was on his phone a lot, and when he wasn't, he was quiet and closed off. Annalise suspected the memories he'd shared with her still had him by the throat.

The tragic event in his life explained a lot…like his affinity for saving children in dangerous hostage situations. It also explained his occasional moodiness when they had been together as a couple.

She wanted to wrap her arms around Evan and somehow comfort him from the bad memories she'd stirred by asking him about Maria. She wanted to somehow take away the guilt she now knew he carried about that tragic loss in his life.

Still, she knew he didn't need her right now. What he really needed was for this case to come to a satisfactory conclusion. He desperately needed to be a hero.

EVAN LEANED BACK in the dining room chair and stretched with his arms overhead. It was just a few minutes after six. He glanced at Annalise, who was sleeping on the sofa.

Telling her about Maria had been one of the most difficult things he'd ever done. He'd spent most of his life trying not to access those painful memories. It had not only been a shameful secret he'd carried, but one that still had the capacity to bring him to his knees.

It had been an event that had forever changed who

he was at the very core. It had stolen his belief that the world was a safe place and had created a self-hatred inside him that had never really gone away.

He'd only told one person about Maria, and that had been Hendrick. He and Hendrick had shared a few too many beers one evening at Evan's house. Hendrick confessed to Evan about being raised in a cult, and Evan had shared his heartache of Maria.

But he needed to put those memories away now. He hated himself for showing Annalise his vulnerability. And in that vulnerable state he'd almost kissed her again.

There was no question there was still something between them, a chemistry…a desire that was difficult to ignore. But he couldn't forget that she'd walked out on him before.

He got up and went into the kitchen to refill his coffee cup. He made a fresh pot of coffee and then poured himself a cup. He took a sip and leaned against the counter. Where was Sadie right now? Had they given her something to eat? Was she sleeping in a car parked on some mountain road? Or was she dead? He shook his head to dispel that particular thought.

Talking about, remembering what had happened to Maria had only made him more desperate than ever to find Sadie. One child at a time, he thought. All he could do was try to save one child at a time.

Part of what had made him a hostage negotiator as an officer of the law before he'd been asked to join TCD was the number of domestic disputes that turned ugly.

Far too often a man locked himself inside a house or apartment with a gun and his children. Most of the time those situations ended with the children being safely released, but occasionally those kinds of hostage situations ended in tragedy.

If Evan could save a child, then it assuaged a tiny piece of the guilt that would forever haunt him, the guilt that he'd been unable to save Maria.

He stretched once again and then grabbed one of the homemade cinnamon rolls that Chief Cummings had given him before he'd left the station after the interviews. It was delicious. At least the chief was correct that his wife definitely knew how to bake.

When he went back into the living room, Annalise was awake. "There's fresh coffee," he said.

"Thanks." She got up and disappeared into the kitchen and returned a moment later with her cup of coffee and one of the cinnamon rolls on a saucer. She sat down next to him at the table.

As they drank their coffee, they talked about the elements of the crime they knew so far. He'd always liked bouncing things off her. Many a night when they were together they'd talk about his work and various crime scenarios.

They talked about his interview with Earl and other potential people at the school who might be involved. They tried to brainstorm where on earth the fugitives might have gone. He talked out all the various investigations that were taking place as she listened and commented.

It was just after eight when a ding sounded from her computer. They both jumped up from the table and hurried to the desk. The page now held another nonsensical sentence.

"It's her," Annalise said, her voice filled with excitement. "It's from Sadie."

"What does it say?"

"It says, 'Miss Annalise, I'm okay.'"

Evan pulled out the desk chair. "Ask her where she is."

Annalise sat and quickly typed out the question.

A moment later Sadie responded. "Cabin," Annalise said. "She says she's in a cabin."

"A cabin where? Is there a name of the place that she can give us? Where is it located?" Evan asked urgently. This was what they'd been waiting for. Thank God the little girl was still alive. Hopefully she could tell them where she was so Evan's team could move in and get her out of there and away from the couple who held her.

He and Annalise stared at the computer screen, waiting for a reply. A minute went by, then another and another. "She must have had to get off the page," Annalise finally said. "I'm just grateful she's still alive."

Hendrick called on Evan's computer. Evan hurried over and answered. "She said she's in a cabin," he told him.

"A cabin? There must be hundreds of cabins in

those mountains," Hendrick said. "I can't do a search without more details. At this moment we don't even know what state they might be in."

"Have you managed to get anything on Winslow's phone yet?"

"Damn, Evan, you know these things take time and a lot of red tape. You've got to have a little patience."

"I'm running out of patience," Evan replied. "If they've put Sadie in front of a computer, then time is running out for her."

"Then let's hope she can get you something more to narrow down a search area," Hendrick replied.

"I'm so scared for her, Evan," Annalise said once the two men had hung up.

He hesitated a moment and then pulled her into his embrace and stroked her hair. The last thing he wanted to do was let her know that he was scared, too.

"Quit screwing around and go to the page I told you to get on," Gretchen said to Sadie.

The girl quickly clicked off the secret page and did as Gretchen asked. The woman scared her. She'd already slapped Sadie twice, once the night before for complaining she was cold and then again this morning for dawdling over breakfast.

The slaps had been hard and when Sadie had cried, Gretchen had threatened to hit her as many times as it took for the girl to stop crying. Sadie had stopped crying on the outside, but she'd cried on the inside for a long time.

Jacob was a little bit nicer; he'd at least given her a pillow to use when she'd gone to bed on the little sofa in the room.

They had driven around on back roads for hours the day before. She'd been so scared, and she was still really scared. Jacob might be nice to her right now, but that didn't mean anything. Gretchen wasn't nice, and she seemed to be the boss. All she'd done since they got to the cabin was yell about how bad things had gone.

She knew they wanted her for a reason, and now she knew why. She understood what they wanted her to do was illegal, and she wasn't even sure she could do it. Miss Annalise had never taught them how to break into places on the internet. Sadie knew if she couldn't do it, then things were going to get bad…really, really bad.

She'd had bad things happen to her before. When she was living in an apartment with her mother before she'd come to the school, there had been many times when Sadie had believed she was going to die.

Sometimes her mother forgot to buy food, and Sadie thought she might starve to death. Other times her mother would beat her until Sadie almost wished she would die. But since being at the school, Sadie didn't want to die. She wanted to go back to the school with her friends and the grown-ups who loved her.

The last thing she'd seen on the private page was

Miss Annalise asking where she was and what the name of the cabin was, but she didn't have the answers.

When they had left the school, they had driven to a place where they had gotten into another car and then they had driven around for a while. They had parked on a road in the middle of nowhere, and then the two grown-ups had taken naps.

She'd stayed awake, worried that a bear might come out of the woods or some other wild animal might attack the car. After they woke up, they started driving again.

Sadie had been asleep when they'd carried her into the small cabin. The curtains were drawn at all the windows, so she hadn't even had a chance to look out.

The only way Miss Annalise and her friend would be able to come and save her was if she could somehow tell them something about the cabin.

What she was scared about was that she wouldn't be able to get Miss Annalise the information before Jacob and Gretchen realized she might not be able to do what they wanted her to do. And once that happened…she truly believed she would be dead.

WHILE THEY WAITED for Sadie to get them more information, Evan was on the phone and checking in on all the progression of the investigation.

Nick was still conducting interviews of the kitchen and housekeeping staff from the school, and Davis and a few other men were at the compound interviewing the members of the Brotherhood of Jacob in an effort to glean more information.

He then contacted Chief Cummings to find out if the tails on Earl had reported anything during the night. So far they had nothing to report. Earl had driven straight home from the police station and hadn't left his house since.

By the time he was finished with all the check-ins, Annalise had made them breakfast. They ate quickly, as if fighting against a ticking time bomb.

Evan had felt the tension before, but Sadie's contact had definitely made him feel like everything was going to explode quickly.

"I still find it hard to believe that Earl is the inside person," Annalise said as they cleared their dishes.

"Right now he's the only one who looks half-way good. Why don't you think he's the one?" Evan asked.

"He is a little reserved, but to be honest," she replied, "I don't want to sound unkind, but I just don't think he's smart enough to put this all together."

"I'm not sure it took a lot of brains to implement this plan. Somebody from the inside told Jacob and Gretchen when would be the best time to break into the school, and that same somebody lifted a key for the garage and one to steal the van."

"I just think the insider is somebody else, somebody we're missing altogether," she replied. "Have you checked out Regina?"

"So far Hendrick hasn't given me anything on her, but we're checking everything," he said.

"I know that." She put their dishes in the dishwasher. "That wasn't me being critical. I know you're in control of everything."

He realized he'd been curt. "Sorry, I didn't mean to snap at you."

She smiled. "I think we're both tense."

He pulled her into his arms and hugged her. "I'm glad you're here with me," he said.

"Me, too," she replied.

For several long moments they simply held each other, and he finally released her. Once again he realized she stirred all kinds of emotions inside him, but there was no way he wanted to examine exactly what they were as long as he was in the middle of this investigation. Right now Sadie needed and deserved all his attention and energy. He returned to his computer, and Annalise sank down at the desk in front of hers.

"Do you really believe Sadie could break into a banking system?" he asked Annalise.

She frowned. "I really don't know. She's brilliant, but I haven't really taught the girls how to do anything like that. She's never been challenged to get through all the security and firewalls that would entail."

"Now that we know she's working a computer, I've got Hendrick watching the banking systems for a breech."

"I just want her to get back to us with more information about where she's being held," Annalise replied. "If she can't do it for them, then she'll be of no use, and that's what scares me for her. She needs to help us find her."

As if her wish was granted, her notification sounded. It was Sadie again.

"She says when she looks out the window, in the distance she sees a big, wooden owl. She believes the name of the cabins has *owl* in it," Annalise told him.

"Does she have any idea where they are located?" Evan asked.

Annalise typed in the question. "She says she doesn't know. She just knows it must be owl something. She also says she doesn't think they had plans to be there."

"So, the odds are good that wherever they are, it isn't a private cabin," Evan said.

They waited several more minutes, but Sadie didn't type anything more. Evan got on a call to Hendrick and told him what Sadie had said.

"I'll start a search right now," Hendrick stated. "Later."

"We're going to get her, aren't we?" Annalise asked, her green eyes shining with a new hope.

"Yeah, I think we're going to get her," he replied. He just hoped they got to her in time. Once again he felt the ticking time bomb inside his veins.

Ticktock.

Chapter Eleven

Two hours later Hendrick called. "Man, I had no idea there were so many cabin resorts around with owl in the name. Owl's Nest, Sleepy Owl, Twin Owls…we're galvanizing local officials to make contact with each one of them to see if Jacob and Gretchen are guests."

"Why would any of them rent to these people who have been splashed across the news for the past twenty-four hours?" Annalise asked.

"Some of these cabins are completely off the grid. The owners or managers might not even know they're harboring fugitives," Hendrick replied. "We've told law enforcement to approach the cabins in unmarked vehicles so we won't spook the fugitives with any police presence."

"So, now it's just a waiting game," Evan replied.

"It's coming to an end. Thank God Sadie got us enough information to narrow the search. I wouldn't be surprised if something pops within the next hour or two."

"Let's hope so. I'm ready to put this one behind me with a happy ending," Evan replied.

"Fingers crossed, it won't be too long now," Hendrick said, and then hung up.

"I should call Chief Cummings and let him know what's going on," Evan said, more to himself than to Annalise.

"Why would you consider not calling him?" she asked.

Evan released a deep sigh. "I don't know. I just fear that if he gets involved in the ultimate take-down, things will somehow get all muddled and screwed up."

"We definitely don't need a screwup at this point," Annalise replied.

"I've got three highly trained men with me. Between the four of us we should be able to take control of a small cabin and two adults who have no warning that we're coming."

"That's got to be your call," she replied.

"I appreciate that. I haven't forgotten that Jacob and Gretchen got away from the school due to Chief Cummings's men and his decision to remove a lot of his men. The last thing I want is for Jacob and Gretchen to somehow escape the cabin, which will result in a manhunt through the mounains. I'm taking a wait and see attitude before I decide to involve Chief Cummings."

And so they waited.

As the minutes and then hours passed, Evan stayed on the phone checking in with the ongoing investigation and Annalise remained at her computer, hoping and praying for a successful end for Sadie.

The tension inside her grew with each minute that ticked by. She wanted to scream, she wanted to cry, she wanted to be in Evan's arms once again.

Spending this time with him had made her realize she wanted to try to rekindle their relationship again. She wanted to reclaim the magic that they once had. But she had no idea if he would ever want to try again with her. She wasn't even sure he'd understood why she had left him in the first place.

She shook her head, aware that she was getting too deep into her emotions about Evan because thoughts of Sadie were too frightening to entertain. Every moment that passed without additional contact with the child made Annalise wonder if she was still alive.

It was just after three when Hendrick called Evan. "We've got them," he said.

"Where?" Evan asked. Annalise got up from the desk and moved to stand just behind him.

"Owl's Nest cabins on mountain road 358. It's about three hours from where you are right now. Local authorities just confirmed with the owner there that they are in cabin number 7. The owner hadn't heard the news of a manhunt. Jacob paid cash for a four-night stay, and the locals are staying on scene with the owner until you all arrive."

"Get me the name of the chief of police in that jurisdiction," Evan said.

"Already got it. It's Chief Joe McCabe," Hendrick replied. "He's expecting your call."

As Annalise listened to Evan talk to Chief Mc-Cabe, her entire body thrummed with excitement. Hopefully in the next four hours or so, Sadie would be safe and Jacob and Gretchen would be under arrest.

"Wish us luck," he said to her when he was off the phone and heading toward the front door.

"You aren't leaving here without me," she protested.

"Annalise, we don't know how this is going to go down. It could get extremely dangerous," he told her.

"I don't care. I'm coming with you whether you like it or not. If I don't ride with you, then I'll take my own car and follow you." She raised her chin in stubbornness.

"Annalise…" he started to protest once again.

She was having none of it. She was going and that was that. There was no way in hell she was staying here. "If you get Sadie out of there, she's going to need to see a familiar face. She'll need me to be there for her," she replied firmly.

He wasn't going to stop her from coming. Sadie would need her…and more than that, she needed to see Sadie. She wanted to hold her tight, to assure herself that the little girl had not only survived physically but emotionally, as well.

"I promise you that if you don't take me with you, then I'll drive on my own," she repeated firmly.

He looked at her for a long moment and then gave

a quick nod. Minutes later they were on the road with Davis driving in a car behind them with Nick and Daniel as passengers.

"I'm almost glad they are out of Chief Cummings's jurisdiction," Evan said as he pressed the gas pedal to pick up speed. "I'll be glad to deliver Jacob and Gretchen to him to put in his jail so he can have all the glory, but I'm fine working with somebody else to take them down."

"I'm just so happy this is finally coming to an end," she replied. "I just want Sadie to be saved."

"I want that, and I also want whoever the insider is behind bars," he replied.

They fell silent as he focused on the road ahead, and Annalise stared out the side window. She could feel his tension in the air, and the last thing she wanted was to be a distraction.

After driving for an hour and a half, he turned onto a narrow road where the trees encroached on either side and stole all the sunshine.

The shadowed semidarkness increased her anxiety. The optimism she'd left her house with waned a bit. It was only going to get darker as evening approached, and things could go so terribly wrong.

What if a gunfight broke out? Would Sadie become collateral damage? Would Evan be hurt? Killed? Her heartbeat quickened. Would Sadie still be alive when they finally got to the cabin? A glance over at Evan let her know he was probably entertaining the same dark thoughts that she was.

His hands clenched the steering wheel, and his

jaw muscles were bunched. He looked like a warrior ready to do battle. All she could do was pray that the warrior would come through on the other side unscathed and that he'd have a living, breathing little girl in his arms.

The small police station was located on a narrow mountain road next to a bar named Whisky Dan's. Evan parked next to another police car in the lot. "Stay here," he said to Annalise. "And lock the doors."

He'd been reluctant to allow her to come along with him, and the only reason he had brought her was because he had no idea how traumatized Sadie might be. He also knew that Annalise would have followed through on her threat to trail the team in her own vehicle. But he had no intention of her being part of the arrest and rescue mission.

He got out of the car and waited for his men to do the same and then the four of them went inside. Chief Joe McCabe greeted them and introduced four of his men. "These guys are as close to a SWAT team as we have," he said.

"We've taken down a lot of men holed up in all kinds of cabins in this area," Officer Larry Knox said.

"A lot of meth-cooking goes on in some of these little cabins," Officer Nash Burton explained.

"The Owl's Nest cabins are owned by Charlie Tankersly. Charlie is something of a character," Chief McCabe said. "He claims to be an artist, and spends most of his time using trash to make things nobody ever buys. But the good news is he supports law and order, and he'll do whatever we ask of him."

"So, let's talk about a plan," Evan said.

For the next forty-five minutes, Evan and Chief McCabe talked about the cabin's location, the best way to approach it and who would do what when they got there.

By the time they left the police station, dusk had fallen, casting the area in deep, purplish shadows. Adrenaline pumped through Evan as he got back into the car where Annalise waited.

"Everything okay?" she asked.

"It's all a go." He started the engine, then waited for his men and the chief's team to load up. They had specific equipment in their vehicle that would hopefully make the takedown easier.

"McCabe seems to have a good team to work with us," he said. "They all seem bright and more than capable, and they're used to taking down people in cabins in this area."

"I just can't wait until this is all over," Annalise replied.

It took twenty minutes before everyone was ready to pull out of the police station parking lot. They would coordinate again a mile from the Owl's Nest cabins.

They had no idea how much firepower the two fugitives had in the cabin. It would be imperative for the agents to use the element of surprise to their advantage.

Evan drove approximately three miles on a road

that was little more than an overgrown trail. How in the hell had the fugitives found this place? It was definitely off the beaten path. Maybe the insider had told them to come to these cabins, knowing they were isolated.

Tree limbs brushed against the side of his car, and what was left of the sunlight was being usurped by both the woods and the encroaching darkness.

Thankfully Annalise remained quiet, allowing him to concentrate on the plan. He stopped his car and the others parked just behind him.

"I don't want you leaving this car for any reason," he said to Annalise. "According to Chief McCabe, the cabin is about a mile up the road." He reached out and touched her cheek. "I need to know you're safe." He pulled his hand back.

"I'll be here waiting for you and Sadie to return," she said softly.

He nodded and then got out of the car. It was cooler here, but he scarcely felt the chill in the air as he clipped his radio to his collar and tuned to the frequency they would all be using.

Chief McCabe opened his trunk, which contained not only a battering ram, but also flash-bang grenades and additional guns and ammo. The men loaded up.

"We want to go in fast and forcefully," Evan said. "But I want everyone to remember that there's a little girl who is their hostage. Whatever we do, we need to get her out of there safe and sound."

"Once we have the fugitives under arrest, I'll

make arrangements with Chief Cummings to transfer them into his custody, but first we need to get them in handcuffs," Chief McCabe said.

"And that's why we're here," Evan replied, eager to get this done and over with. The fact that within minutes this could all be over was exhilarating. The thought that within minutes it could all go terribly wrong also flashed in his head.

"Shall we coordinate our watches?" Davis asked.

Evan's blood cooled and his nerves settled down, the way they always did before going into battle. Finally they were all ready to go. They moved through the woods like silent, stealthy shadows.

Chief McCabe was not only in contact with all members of the team, but also with Charlie in the owner's cabin. Thankfully the cabins were all some distance away from each other, and Charlie assured them that he wouldn't get in their way.

When the small cabin where Jacob and Gretchen were holed up came into view, Evan halted just behind a large tree. Some of the others found similar hiding places while a few of them circled around to the back of the cabin.

A red Ford Escort was parked out front, and while Evan was eager to find out who it belonged to, his first priority was getting Gretchen and Jacob arrested and Sadie out of there.

This was it. This was the culmination of all the hard work of dozens of agents. They were either going to get it right, or they'd completely screw it up and somehow the fugitives would escape once again.

They couldn't let that happen. They had to control the scene. He had to control it. If he somehow lost control of things, then another little girl might die.

The curtains were drawn in the cabin's windows. Charlie had said the cabin the fugitives occupied consisted of a small living room–kitchenette area and a bedroom and a bath.

Evan gripped his gun more firmly. He mentally counted down from three, and when he reached one, he whispered into his radio. "Move in, let's move in."

He watched as the two men manning the battering ram took their position at the front door. He and Davis moved to stand just behind them while the rest of the men surrounded the cabin, ready to go into the two windows on the back side.

Thankfully the front door didn't look that solid. It was old and weathered and should be breached fairly easy. The minute it was possible, Davis and Evan would sweep in and hopefully this all would go down without a single shot fired.

"On the count of three," he now said into the radio. "One…two…three."

Boom. They hit the door with tremendous force, cracking it right down the middle. Davis and Evan swept in. "Get on the floor, get down on the floor. Facedown and hands on the back of your heads," Evan yelled.

At the same time, the sound of breaking windows came from the back, and within seconds Nick and one of McCabe's men flew into the living room.

The couple cursed. They were seated at the table, but seeing they were outgunned and outmanned, they did as Evan asked and got on the floor.

"This was all his idea," Gretchen said. "He told me he'd kill me if I didn't go along with him. He's… he's so abusive. He beats me."

"You stinking traitor," Jacob yelled. "This was all her idea. She planned it all."

"Stop talking," Evan commanded as he watched the two of them being patted down for weapons by Nick. Once it was confirmed neither of them had a weapon on them, they were jerked up to their feet and handcuffed.

Evan turned to see Sadie curled up in the corner of a nasty-looking brown sofa. Her eyes were huge as she watched everything that was happening. Thank God she was alive and appeared unharmed.

"Hi, Sadie," he said to her with a smile. He crouched in front of her. "Do you know who I am?"

"You're Miss Annalise's friend. I saw you on her phone. Are you here to take me out of this place?"

"We're here to take you out of here."

She nodded. "Good. I really didn't want to do what they wanted me to do."

"Honey, it's over now and those people are out of your life forever," Evan replied, just grateful that she appeared to be okay. "Are you ready to come outside with me? Miss Annalise has been really worried about you, and she can't wait to see you and tell you how smart and how very brave you have been."

"Did you get Miss Annalise something to eat?

Last time I was with her, her tummy was really growling because she was so hungry."

Evan stared at the beautiful child with her innocent blue eyes and felt utterly humbled. After being kidnapped and brought to this seedy cabin, that her first thought would be of her teacher being hungry spoke of how very special this child was.

"Yes, Miss Annalise has been fed several times," he replied. "Come on, let's get you out of here."

She got off the sofa and placed her little hand in his with utter trust. Together they left the cabin, and he used a flashlight to guide them back toward his car.

They walked for a little ways and then, sensing that Sadie was growing weary, he pulled her up in his arms. "I hope we didn't scare you when we burst into the cabin," he said.

"I was way more scared that Gretchen was going to kill me," she replied. "She's really, really mean."

"We weren't going to let that happen. Now she and Jacob will go to jail for a very long time."

"That's good. They aren't nice people," she said, and tightened her thin arms around his neck.

They were several feet in front of the car when Annalise finally saw them. She got out of the vehicle and ran toward them.

"Sadie," she cried.

"Miss Annalise!"

Evan set the little girl on the ground and teacher and student raced to each other. When Annalise reached Sadie, she fell to her knees and opened her arms wide.

Tears poured down Annalise's face as she hugged Sadie close. As Evan watched the two of them, he couldn't help the lump of emotion that rose in his throat.

He allowed the reunion to go on for several long moments before he finally spoke again. "I've got to go back. You two get into the car, lock the doors and I'll be back here as soon as I can."

He waited until the two got into the backseat, and then he turned and hurried back toward the cabin.

Finally, it was almost over. Two bad guys were in custody and his young hostage was safe. Considering how it all could have gone wrong, the actual takedown had been surprisingly easy and rather anticlimactic, not that he was complaining. Before he reached the cabin, he pulled his phone from his pocket and connected to Hendrick.

"We got them," he said once the tech appeared.

"And Sadie?" Hendrick asked.

"Safe and in my car."

"Thank God. Then my naked dance with torches burning and the sacrifice of a corn dog worked," Hendrick said with a wicked grin.

"You've always hated corn dogs," Evan replied.

"Okay, so that was an easy sacrifice," Hendrick replied.

Evan laughed, and it felt so good to finally reach this point and be able to laugh. "I just wanted you to know that this part of the ordeal is over." His smile faded. "But we still need to identify the person who aided and abetted these criminals."

Hendrick nodded. "You don't believe Earl Winslow is your man?"

Evan hesitated. "I can't be positive, but my gut is telling me he isn't the insider. I've got to go. We've still got a lot to finish up here."

"I'll keep digging into backgrounds, and I'll talk to you later."

Evan returned to the cabin where the two fugitives were not only handcuffed but also had their ankles bound, making it impossible for them to run.

The officers had rounded up a total of three automatic long guns and two handguns. Along with the weapons was enough ammunition to ward off a small army. Thank God they had been taken down without incident.

Chief McCabe smiled at Evan. "If you want to take off, I can assure you my men will process the scene and send you all the reports and evidence we collect."

"Thanks, and I really appreciate your cooperation in working with us on this," Evan replied. "It's been a pleasure."

"Glad we could help," Chief McCabe replied, and the two men shook hands. "We'll make sure these two are transferred successfully into Chief Cummings's custody. They have far more serious charges to face in that jurisdiction than in ours."

Evan remained for another thirty minutes or so and then returned to the car where Annalise and

Sadie waited. "How are you doing?" he asked when he was behind the steering wheel.

"We're good," Annalise said. "I've been telling her how smart she was in helping us find her."

"Sadie, you've been amazing," Evan said. "You asked me if Miss Annalise had eaten, but you didn't tell me if you had eaten."

"Gretchen made me some macaroni and cheese, but the macaroni was really crunchy and it wasn't very good," Sadie replied.

"How about when we see a fast-food place on the way home we stop and get you a big cheeseburger and fries," Evan said.

"That would be awesome," Sadie replied. "And maybe a chocolate shake?"

Annalise laughed. "You got it."

Once they were on the road home, the two passengers in the back fell asleep. Evan found himself glancing in his rearview mirror and gazing at Annalise.

Without the pressure of the fugitives now burning in his brain, his emotions where Annalise was concerned came to the surface.

He was still in love with her. He realized now he'd never stopped loving her. She had surprised him with her strength throughout this ordeal. He wasn't sure if she wanted another chance with him or not, but more important he wasn't sure he would ever trust her with his heart again.

Chapter Twelve

It was just after midnight when Evan finally pulled into Annalise's driveway. They had gotten Sadie a fast-food child's meal on the way home, and her resident attendant was now with her at the hospital where she would be thoroughly checked out before returning to her room at the school.

Annalise knew her time with Evan was drawing to an end. With Sadie found, Evan had no reason to stay in town. Whatever was left of the investigation could be handled in Knoxville.

"I'm so glad that Sadie seems to be okay mentally and the whole ordeal didn't break her spirit," she said once they were in her living room.

"Thank goodness. She's definitely a special girl," Evan replied.

"She is," Annalise agreed. She cast him a surreptitious gaze and wondered if he was thinking about another special little girl named Maria. "Are you tired?"

"I am, but at the moment I'm waiting for the last of my adrenaline to burn off."

"Surely you aren't planning on packing up and leaving here this late tonight," she said.

"Actually I was hoping I could avail myself of your hospitality and spend one more night here, then head out sometime tomorrow," he replied. "In fact I'm thinking about that bed in the guest room."

She smiled at him. "It's all yours. I'd say you've more than earned it."

They engaged in small talk about the case as they lounged on the sofa. "I'm sure you're ready to get back to your own life," he said.

"Almost." She would probably not have another chance to talk to him about her feelings. The time was now, before he packed up and left her house. "Evan, I'm still in love with you."

Her words hung in the air. He stared at her for a long moment and then looked down at the coffee table. "Annalise," he protested softly, "isn't it better to just leave things alone between us?"

"No, it's not." She gazed at him and her heart began to pound with every emotion from anxiety to love. "I want another chance with you, Evan. I've never stopped loving you, and having this time with you only confirms to me that you're the only man I want in my life."

He frowned and his eyes darkened. "You walked away from me easily enough three years ago. In fact, as I remember, you sent me a text to tell me goodbye…a text for God's sake."

"Walking away from you was the most difficult decision I've ever made in my life," she replied.

"And I sent you a goodbye text because I knew if I tried to say goodbye to you in person, I wouldn't leave you."

She leaned toward him. "Evan, I told you that I was unhappy a million times. I told you that you were being too controlling and I was losing my sense of self. I complained that you ran our relationship like one of your hostage negotiations."

He remained silent, his eyes dark and shuttered, and still she continued. "Evan, I didn't want to take that job so far away from you, but I'd reached the point where I wasn't even sure you would care if I left you or not. Each time I tried to talk to you, you were so emotionless and you'd withdraw from me. I didn't want Evan the calm and skillful negotiator in my life. I needed Evan the man to give me a reason to stay… Tell me to stay now, Evan. Tell me you are willing to give me another chance."

A nerve pulsed in his strong jawline. "What makes you think it would work between us now?"

The question made hope leap into her heart. "Because I know more about you now, because I understand you better and I'm a stronger person than I was three years ago. We can make it this time, Evan. Please give me…give us a second chance."

She saw a softness in his eyes, and she grabbed his hand with hers. "I've thought about you every single day that passed. I… I kept hoping you would call me."

He jerked his hand from hers and stood up. "Call you? Do you have any idea how much you wrecked me? Annalise, I believed in you…in us…and if I couldn't trust you, then who could I trust? If I was too controlling, then we should have talked about it, but you just gave up on us. I don't remember you trying too hard to tell me what you were feeling at the time."

She saw his pain in the depths of his eyes…felt it emanating from him. "I wasn't strong enough, Evan. I admit I was weak, and it was difficult for me to talk to you about these sensitive subjects, but I can't go back and do things differently." She got up from the sofa, as well. "All we have is the future, and I know we can get this right."

He raised a hand and rubbed the back of his neck as he broke eye contact with her. "I'm afraid, Annalise," he finally said softly. "I'm afraid to give you my heart again, and then if you get unsure you just send me a text and walk away. Now I'm exhausted and I really need to get some sleep."

Without saying another word, he turned and walked down the hallway toward the guest room. She watched him until he disappeared from her sight, and then she collapsed back on the sofa as tears burned at her eyes.

She'd hoped…she'd so desperately wanted… But apparently it didn't matter what she wanted because he wasn't willing to try again. She felt so much better prepared to have a relationship with him now. She had been weak before when it came to confronting him about her feelings. She'd not only been unfair to him, but also to herself by not being strong enough to talk to him about the important things in their relationship.

Maybe in the morning she'd have a chance to talk with him one more time before he left her house. Maybe once he was better rested his heart would open to her again. A tiny flicker of hope filled her heart.

They were both exhausted tonight. It had not been a good time for her to talk to him about all this. She should have waited until they both had gotten plenty of sleep and the crime situation was truly behind them.

With renewed hope still burning in her heart, she swiped the tears from her eyes and got up from the sofa. She was exhausted, as well. There had been far too little sleep in the past forty-eight hours.

She went into her bedroom and changed from her jeans and T-shirt into a black nightshirt. She hadn't realized just how exhausted she was until her familiar mattress seemed to embrace her. The minute she closed her eyes she was asleep and dreaming of being in Evan's arms once again.

As exhausted as Evan was, he couldn't stop the thoughts that kept sleep at bay. Hearing that Annalise still loved him had filled him with a tremendous joy until old memories of hurt and loss had intruded.

Was he willing to put his heart on the line with her once again? There was no question that she wasn't the same woman she'd been when they'd been together. She was better. There was a confidence, a strength that flowed from her eyes that he found sexy as hell.

Had he been controlling in their previous relationship? Probably. He'd controlled her in an effort to keep her safe, to make sure she didn't wind up in an alley with a knife to her throat.

He frowned and blinked at that thought. It was the first time he realized how those moments in an alley when he'd been eight years old had affected him his entire life. He'd had no control when Maria had been stolen away. Was it possible he'd been trying to get that control back through his relationship with Annalise, a woman he had deeply loved?

He finally fell into a deep sleep. The ringing of a video call suddenly awakened him. He glanced at the clock on the nightstand and realized he'd been asleep for only about an hour. Why would Hendrick be calling him now? Did he have some information about the insider?

He turned on the lamp on the nightstand and grabbed his phone. "This better be good," he said with a grin at his friend.

Hendrick didn't return the smile. "Evan, Jacob has escaped from the jail in Pearson."

Shock electrified Evan, and for a moment he was sure he'd misunderstood what Hendrick had said. "What?" Evan swung his legs over the side of the bed. "When?"

"About thirty minutes ago."

"How did this happen?" Evan asked, still stunned

by the news. He stood and grabbed a pair of his black slacks and pulled them on.

"The transfer of the prisoners was made successfully by two of Chief McCabe's men. Jacob was locked in a cell by himself, and thirty minutes later somehow he just walked out."

"Is there a camera in the jail?"

"Apparently there's only one camera, and it hasn't been functional for about a month or so."

"What kind of rundown facility is Chief Cummings running?" Evan yanked on a shirt. "Did anyone see where he went when he just walked out? Did he get into a waiting car or was he on foot?"

"Right now I have no more information other than he's out."

"What about Gretchen?"

"She's still behind bars," Hendrick replied.

Evan's frustration shot through the roof. Damn it, they'd all done their jobs and gotten the two behind bars. Jacob was a dangerous man, and now he was out on the streets once again and who knew what he might do.

"Does anyone have any idea where he might be headed?"

"Maybe back to his compound. As you know, the men stationed there were pulled off when you got the two into custody."

Evan cursed once again. "I'll call Chief Cummings and find out exactly what's going on and what he's doing to get Jacob back into custody."

"I know he sent out an alert. That's how I found

out about it. Let me know if there's anything I can do to help from this end," Hendrick said.

"Will do." Evan disconnected the phone.

He quickly grabbed his socks and shoes. He couldn't believe this was happening. Jacob would be more dangerous than ever now, and who knew what resources he might be able to tap into now that he was out and on the run.

When he had his shoes on, he called Chief Cummings, who answered on the first ring. "You heard," he said.

"Just now," Evan replied. "I wanted to check to make sure you have somebody stationed at the compound so Jacob can't go back there."

"Already done, and there will be a full investigation into exactly what happened at the jail."

Evan wanted to rail at the man about his department and all the epic fails, but he didn't. In the end it wouldn't solve anything, and at the moment he still needed to work with these local officials to get the fugitive back into custody.

"Did anyone see him walk out of the building? Is there anyone who can tell us whether he left on foot or had a vehicle waiting for him?" he asked.

"So far we haven't found a witness. I was in the station with just a skeleton crew, but I'll be investigating the situation. He had no access to a phone while he was in custody so I'm guessing he's on foot. I have dozens of patrolmen looking for him as we speak."

"You'll keep me updated?" Evan asked.

"Of course," Chief Cummings replied.

At least Nick, Davis and Daniel hadn't left town yet. His next phone call was to Davis. "Unpack your bags, we're not out of here yet." He explained the situation and told him to update the other two agents and then wait for further instructions.

They needed to find Jacob quickly and get him off the streets before he managed to kill somebody else. Who knew what kind of resources he could get to with a simple phone call to one of his followers? Most of them would do anything to help their leader.

He put his holster back on and then opened his bedroom door, surprised to see the living room lights on. Apparently Annalise hadn't been able to sleep.

He thought he heard a deep male voice. Was she listening to the television? He stepped into the hall-way and pulled his gun, the hackles on the back of his neck standing up.

Gripping his gun firmly, he slowly walked down the hall and stepped into the living room. He swallowed a gasp. Annalise stood before him, her face radiating sheer terror. Jacob stood behind her, one arm wrapped around her waist, the other pointing a gun at her head.

"Ah, the man we were just coming to find," Jacob said with a smile. "Put your gun down."

"Why are you here, Jacob? What do you want?" Evan asked, his heart beating an unsteady rhythm. He did not obey Jacob's command. There was no way in hell he was going to put down his weapon.

In a million years he couldn't have foreseen Jacob coming here. How did the man even know where Annalise lived? How had he gotten here? He had assumed Jacob would want to get as far away from town as possible.

The utter terror shining from Annalise's eyes made a red hot rage well up inside him. He tamped it down. He had to keep his cool in this situation, and drew in several breaths in an effort to regulate his racing heartbeat.

This wasn't like facing a frightened Phil who he had assumed wasn't likely to use his gun. Jacob had already proven that he could kill in cold blood.

"Put your gun down," Jacob repeated, and yanked Annalise closer to him. She gasped, and tears began to run down her cheeks.

"I can't do that," Evan replied. "Just tell me why you're here. What is it you want from me?"

"I want you to bring me Sadie."

Evan looked at him in surprise. Did Jacob really believe he could still get the little girl to break into the banking system and steal a bunch of money? Was he so far out of touch with reality that he truly believed he could still follow through on his scheme?

"You need to let Annalise go before you and I can have a serious talk," Evan replied.

Jacob caressed her cheek with the barrel of the gun and then brought it back up to the side of her head. "I'm not letting her go until I get Sadie."

Evan wanted to rip the man's throat out for what he was doing to Annalise. "Don't you get it, man?

We all know what your intentions were, and it's over. All your men are either dead or in jail."

"It's not over," Jacob screamed. "All I need is that kid, and then when she does what I want, I'll leave the country. I'll be someplace where nobody can ever touch me."

"Even if I bring Sadie here, it's still all over," Evan replied. "You'll never be able to board a plane. Officers all over the country will be looking for you."

"Money talks, and with enough money I can buy a plane and my own pilot. Now, if you don't bring me Sadie, then I'm going to shoot your girlfriend."

Evan's stomach tied itself in knots. In all the hostage negotiations he'd ever been through, his emotions had never been so out of control as at this moment. "She's not my girlfriend. She doesn't mean anything to me. If you kill her, then I'm going to kill you. She'll be dead but so will you. Now, let her go and put your gun down," Evan demanded.

As he was talking, he was seeking any kind of weakness he could exploit to either talk the man down or take him down physically.

At the moment he saw absolutely no weakness, and that scared the hell out of him.

ANNALISE'S HEART BEAT frantically and so fast it felt like it might explode right out of her chest. She'd never been so frightened in her entire life.

She'd awakened and had been unable to go back

to sleep. She'd gotten up to get a drink of water, and Jacob had come up behind her in the kitchen.

The cold barrel of his gun now dug into the side of her head, and she was terrified with each moment that passed that Jacob would pull the trigger. At this point he certainly had nothing to lose.

She understood that while Evan would not want her to be killed, his ultimate goal had to be to stop Jacob here and now. If he did his job, he would never give into Jacob's demands and she might be another…she might be the last tragic victim to Jacob's madness.

The burly man smelled of rancid sweat and complete evil, and all she wanted was to get away from him. But with the gun to her head there wasn't much she could do except weep silent, helpless tears.

"Jacob, put the gun down and let her go," Evan said calmly.

"Get me that kid," Jacob bellowed, and tightened his arm around Annalise.

"That's not happening," Evan replied. "You need to end this now, Jacob. You need to put your gun down and face the consequences of your actions."

This was a standoff that had her life in the balance. She knew Evan wasn't going to yield and put his gun down, and Jacob seemed determined not to give himself up.

She'd never felt as helpless as she did right now. Jacob was too strong to fight against, and the longer this went on the more she was certain he was going to shoot her.

Mentally she prepared herself to die. She said a silent goodbye to her parents and hoped they would be okay without her. And she said goodbye to Evan, sorry for the three years that had been wasted when they hadn't been together.

Suddenly she knew there was really only one thing she could do. It was definitely a risk. It might not work, but she had to do something to try to save herself. She gazed at Evan, the man she would always love, the last man she might ever see, and then she opened her mouth and screamed.

She screamed as loud as she could, knowing it was one of the things Jacob hated. "Stop that," the big man yelled. For a brief moment, the gun slipped from her head and his hold on her loosened. She immediately fell to her knees, and as she squeezed her eyes tightly closed, two shots nearly deafened her.

Oh God, who had been shot? When she stopped screaming, she heard Jacob cursing from someplace behind her. Then strong hands grabbed her by the shoulders and pulled her up to her feet.

She opened her eyes and saw Evan's beautiful face. "Come on, let's get you away from him."

He pointed her toward the sofa and while she sank down, he approached Jacob, who was lying on the floor. Blood gushed from a wound in his chest, and he held both hands over it.

Evan stepped over Jacob and grabbed the gun that the man had apparently dropped when he'd been shot and had fallen backward. Evan then got on his phone and called Chief Cummings. "I need an ambulance at Annalise's house. I just shot Jacob."

"On it," the chief said.

Evan hung up and then called Nick. "I need the three of you to get to Annalise's house. I want you to escort Jacob to the hospital and stay with him until he's well enough to be put in federal lockdown. I do not want him going back into local custody."

As Evan made his arrangements, Annalise shivered on the sofa. She was utterly traumatized by what had just happened. From the moment Jacob had grabbed her in the kitchen until this time she'd been so afraid that she'd get shot or that Evan would be killed.

Now a sickness bordering nausea twisted in her stomach and she'd never been so cold in her life. She continued to shiver as the emergency vehicles arrived along with Chief Cummings and Evan's teammates.

It wasn't until the ambulance finally left and everyone else was gone that Evan walked over to her and pulled her up and into his arms.

He didn't say a word, he just held her tight. She clung to him as emotion began to choke her. "I… I just wanted a drink of water," she said through her tears. "I came into the k-kitchen and suddenly he was right on me. I… I really thought he was going to kill me…kill us."

Evan tightened his arms around her. "I've never been so terrified in my life."

She raised her head and looked at him in surprise. "Really? But you seemed so calm and in control."

"Oh, baby, I was so afraid that I was going to mess up, and I'd have never forgiven myself if anything would have happened to you." He tightened his arms around her. "It's over now. He'll never hurt you again. He's never going to hurt anyone ever again."

"Thank God," she whispered. She continued to weep for several more minutes, and then finally she released her death grip around his neck and stepped back from him. "I'm sorry," she said as she swiped at her tears. "I've just never been so frightened in my entire life."

"You were amazing under pressure." His gaze warmed her. "By screaming and then dropping to your knees, you gave me the shot I needed. Thank God his shot went wild." He pointed to a hole in the far wall.

"When we were in the school, he told us over and over again that he hated whining and screaming," she replied. "It was the only thing I could think of to do."

"It was absolutely brilliant," he replied. He led her back to the sofa where they both sat. "Chief Cummings is coming back to get our official report. Just tell him exactly what happened."

She nodded and drew several steadying breaths. "Do you think he would have killed me?"

He hesitated a long moment. "Yeah," he finally said. "I think eventually he might have, but I was looking for a shot before that happened. Thank God your scream surprised him and shook him up."

It was the longest night of her life. Chief Cummings finally returned to take their statements, and he brought with him a loaf of pumpkin spice bread his wife had baked.

Jacob had come through the patio door, and Annalise was horrified to realize when she'd stepped out on the deck earlier she didn't remember locking the door behind her. She'd given a killer easy access to her.

Finally it was all over. The terror, the official statements…everything. "Let's see if now we can get some much-needed sleep," Evan said.

Together they walked down the hallway. "Evan—" she turned to him when they reached the doorway to the guest room "—I promise I won't expect anything from you…but could you sleep with me? Could you just hold me in your arms?"

"I can do that," he said softly.

Once they reached her room, Evan kicked off his shoes and socks, took off his slacks and shirt and then crawled into bed with her and pulled her into an embrace.

It was the first time she'd felt completely safe since the school had been taken over by gunmen. "Just think, we can get up in the morning and have pumpkin spice bread with our coffee," he murmured drowsily in her ear.

"Why does he keep giving you baked goods?"

"He told me his wife loves to bake. He mentioned

she'd grown up in foster care and that she loved to bake to take her mind off the terrible existence she had there."

"It's funny, his wife went through foster care and married a policeman and Gretchen went through foster care and became a criminal," she said sleepily.

And then she knew no more.

Chapter Thirteen

Evan awoke first. He was spooned around Annalise, and she was still sleeping soundly. For a moment he remained unmoving and simply reveled in the feel of her warm body.

He finally slid from the bed, grateful he hadn't awakened her. After grabbing his clothes off the floor, he went into the guest room to grab clean ones, then took a quick hot shower in the guest bathroom.

Once Evan was dressed, he went into the kitchen and put on a pot of coffee. He'd slept soundly, but had awakened with a lot of things on his mind, like who the inside man or woman might be.

Once he had a cup of coffee before him at the dining room table, he called Hendrick. He told him his thoughts, then asked the tech agent to do several things.

"Are you sure?" Hendrick asked with surprise when Evan had finished.

"I'm positive," Evan said. "Get back to me as soon as you have some information for me."

"You'll be the first person I tell," Hendrick said, and then hung up.

Evan then called Director Pembrook and explained to her what he was thinking and what he believed. She told him to gather the facts and let her know if he needed any other resources.

He sipped his coffee slowly as the thoughts whirling in his head made him half-crazy. If he was wrong, then he'd be destroying an innocent person's life. But if he was right, then the rat would be caught before Evan left town later today.

He got up and headed over to Annalise's desk. In the second drawer he found what he needed—a blank piece of white paper. He carried it and a ball-point pen back to the table.

Sometimes he needed to write things down in order to straighten out his chaotic thoughts, and at the moment he definitely needed to write down what was in his head and then take a good, hard look at it all.

He'd been at it for about twenty minutes when Annalise came into the room. She had obviously showered and was dressed in a pair of jeans and a pink T-shirt that enhanced the green of her eyes.

She greeted him with a bright smile. "Good morning," she said and then beelined for the coffee.

"Back at you," he replied.

She got a cup of coffee and then sank into a chair across from him. "I wasn't sure if you'd be gone this morning or not."

"I'm tying up some last-minute things, but I'll get

a flight out of here this evening. I hope you don't mind me hanging out here until then."

"Of course not," she replied. For a long moment she held his gaze, and he could see love shining there. There was not only unfinished business concerning the crime, but he knew now there was still more unfinished business with her.

"What are you doing?" she asked, and gestured to the piece of paper before him.

"Last night before you went to sleep, you said something that made me realize I'd overlooked something...something that should have been checked out before now."

"And what's that?"

"The fact that both Chief Cummings's wife and Gretchen were in foster care," he replied.

She looked at him with a frown. "What does that have to do with anything?"

"Maybe nothing, or maybe everything. I'm waiting for Hendrick to confirm something for me."

Annalise stared at him. "Are you telling me you think Chief Cummings's wife is our insider?"

He smiled at her grimly. "I think she's definitely a piece of the puzzle, but I now believe Chief Cummings is the mastermind."

She gasped in surprise. "Are you sure?"

"I'm looking at the factual evidence and adding my own suppositions," he replied.

"Tell me." She leaned forward with interest.

It was like old times...the good old times. She

had always been one of his best sounding boards, and he knew today would be no different.

He looked down at what he'd written. "The first thing is Chief Cummings told me that Bert Epstein was one of his best friends. Being friendly with the security guard might have given Walter not only the information as to who would be in the school at a certain time, but also access to the van and garage keys."

"Okay, what else?" she asked.

"The night that Jacob and Gretchen escaped, Walter had pulled off a lot of his men from guard duty at the back of the school."

"Keep going," Annalise said.

Funny, he knew what he'd written down was solid, but it made him feel better that she hadn't rejected anything he'd said so far.

"Walter was at the jail when Jacob walked out," he continued. "And Walter knew where you lived, and how else would Jacob know to come here? I wouldn't be surprised if Walter was the one who drove him here."

She leaned back in her chair. "My God, Evan. When it's laid out like that, he looks guilty as hell. And when the ultimate takedown occurred, it was a complete success without Walter's involvement. So what happens next?"

"I'm waiting for some additional information from Hendrick and then we're going to get an arrest warrant. I believe I have enough circumstantial evidence to take him down. And once we get his phone records, I believe they'll prove without a shadow of a doubt that he's our man. It will be my pleasure to arrest that bastard."

She reached out and covered his hand with hers. "I always knew you were the best hostage negotiator in the world, but you're also a brilliant FBI agent, as well." She squeezed his hand and then released it.

"I don't know about that. If I was that brilliant, I would have seen all of this before now. Each incident taken separately I managed to overlook, but this morning it all came together."

"So, did anyone interview Jacob? And did he say anything about Walter being behind all this, or is he even able to be interviewed?"

"Oh, he was able. The gunshot wound was not life-threatening and he was interviewed extensively last night. But he refused to cooperate in any way. He probably thinks Walter is going to somehow get him out of this again."

"Then he's really delusional," she replied. "What about Gretchen? Is she talking?"

"Not a word except to cuss anyone who asks her anything," he replied. "Although when we arrested them she insisted that she was an abused woman and was terrified of Jacob."

"Trust me, there's no way she was abused or terrified. She had no problems beating the crap out of me."

"I hate that you went through that," he said, her words generating new anger at the person he believed had helped those people get into the school in the first place.

His phone rang with an incoming video call. "Hey, man. What do you have for me?" he asked Hendrick.

"Gretchen Owens was in foster care from the age of six when her mother gave her up. She bounced around among several foster homes, but when she was fifteen she was fostered by Jackie and Damon Huck and she remained with them until she aged out," he said.

"And Chief Cummings's wife?" Evan asked.

"Rose Mayfield entered the foster care system when she was eight. Her parents were killed in a car accident, and there were no other relatives to take her in. She was with the same foster parents until she was fourteen and, due to health issues, they had to give her back to the state. She was then placed with Jackie and Damon Huck until she aged out."

"Bingo," Evan said. "Thanks, Hendrick."

"I've got your warrant ready, and I'm faxing it to you right now. You have the full approval and authority of Director Pembrook and the support of the department behind you. Call me on the other side."

Evan got the documents he needed and then sat back down at the table.

"So, when is this all going down?" she asked.

"Soon. I'm just waiting for Davis and my other men to come and get me." He grinned at her. "It's questionable what role Chief Cummings's wife played in all this, but I have every confidence that

Walter is the insider and this will finally put this case to bed."

As if on cue, Annalise's doorbell rang. Evan's backup had arrived. For the next thirty minutes, the men sat at the table and talked about their game plan, which was really quite simple. Go in, take him down and get out.

"I know he's at the station right now," Evan said. "I have no interest in embarrassing him by a take-down in front of his men. Hopefully we can take care of business in his office and then escort him out of there peacefully and without handcuffs."

"And if he doesn't go along with that plan?" Davis asked.

"Then all bets are off," Evan said firmly. He stood up from the table. "Let's all rock and roll."

The three agents left the house, then Annalise walked with Evan to the door. "I can feel your ex-citement," she said. "Go get your man, Evan, and be safe while you do it."

He smiled and then grabbed her in his arms and kissed her long and hard. When he released her, he immediately turned and went out of the house.

ALL OF THEM were jazzed on the drive to the Pearson police station. "I can't believe this bastard was play-ing us all along," Davis said from the passenger seat.

"He obviously made a deal with the devil and now there's hell to pay," Daniel said from the back-seat.

They all continued to talk about the case until

Evan turned into the police station parking lot. Then they fell into a sober silence.

Evan got out of the car with a sense of purpose. He knew he was right about this. Not only did his gut tell him he was right, but the circumstantial evidence all supported it. He was also certain more evidence would come to light that would prove him right.

"Well, well, if it isn't the G-men," the chief said as they entered the building. "Come to tell us good-bye before you leave town?" He stood with two of his patrolmen just behind the reporting counter.

"Just tying up some final things. Could we talk to you in your office?" Evan asked.

"Sure, come on back." He gestured for them to follow him into a small office with a desk and two chairs before it. "I'll tell one of my boys to bring in a couple more chairs," he said.

"Oh, that won't be necessary," Evan replied. "We won't be here long." He pulled the arrest warrant out of his pocket and tossed it on top of the desk.

"What's this?" Walter asked with a frown. He picked up the paperwork.

"It's a warrant for your arrest on a variety list of charges including conspiracy to commit murder and kidnapping, just to name a few," Evan replied.

"The hell you say." Walter looked at him in shock and threw the paperwork back on the desk. "Is this come kind of a joke?"

"It's no joke, Walter," Evan replied.

"You aren't taking me anywhere. This is all a

big mistake," Walter said, and then made a move toward his gun.

Davis, Nick and Daniel drew their weapons. "Whoa." Walter raised his hands above his waist. "I'm telling you this is all some kind of a terrible mistake."

"Walter, I need you to give me your weapon and your cell phone," Evan said.

"I'm telling you this is a load of crap." Walter's face flushed red. "I'm the chief of the police around here, not some damn criminal. You got this all wrong."

"You'll have a chance to defend yourself in a court of law," Davis said. He continued to tell Walter his rights under the law.

"Walter, we can escort you out of here quietly without handcuffs, or we'll do it the hard way. We don't want to cause any drama in your police station, so why don't you give me your gun and your phone and we'll escort you out of here without the cuffs," Evan said.

Walter held Evan's gaze for a long moment, and then sighed and appeared to crumple within himself. "Do you have any idea how much they pay me as a civil servant? I got tired of working my ass off to make small-town wages. Nobody was supposed to get killed."

He placed his gun and cell phone on the desk and then straightened. "I'd prefer to walk out of here without handcuffs."

They all walked out together, and Walter was

placed in the backseat between Daniel and Nick. "I suppose Jacob is singing like a bird. I should have never trusted an idiot like him to begin with," Walter said. "He's the one who killed people…he and his crazy wife."

"We have agents in the area heading to your house to arrest your wife, as well," Davis said.

Walter straightened. "Please, she had absolutely nothing to do with this. I did it all. I knew she was friendly with Gretchen, and I knew Gretchen was married to Jacob. Rose didn't do anything wrong. She was always trying to counsel Gretchen to do good things in her life, but Gretchen is a bad seed."

"Then your wife should be able to prove her innocence in a court of law," Nick said.

Walter fell silent and so did the others. Hendrick contacted Evan with a meeting point for other federal agents to take custody of Walter and take him to a facility where he would be arraigned and await trial.

Once that was done, Davis dropped Evan back at Annalise's place. He remained on the front porch for several minutes. With the crime completely cleared up, he had nothing left but his feelings for the woman who had been by his side throughout the whole ordeal.

He had one final phone call to make, and then he knocked on her door and she opened it. "Thank God you're safe and sound," she said as she gestured him inside.

"Everything went smoothly, and Walter and his wife are now in custody."

"So, your work here is done," she replied as the two of them sank down on the sofa.

"Not quite."

She looked at him quizzically. "What's left?"

He reached out and took one of her hands in his. "Annalise, you asked me if you could have a second chance, but I've been thinking and I've realized it's me who should be asking you for a second chance."

He squeezed her hand tightly. "I screwed up, Annalise. I didn't listen to you when you were telling me you were unhappy. I was too controlling because I was afraid I'd lose you. I was so afraid you'd be another person I loved with all my heart who would disappear and I'd never know what happened to you. I need you to give me a second chance to get it right. I love you. I've never stopped loving you."

"Oh, Evan." She leaned forward and he captured her lips with his. This was the woman he wanted by his side. He wanted to brainstorm crimes with her. He wanted to cheer her on no matter where she worked or what she did, and he wanted to end each day with her in his arms.

"We owe ourselves a second chance," she said when the kiss ended. "There's way too much love between us to let it go."

"I'm not letting it go. I'm not letting you go. I promise you this time around we'll get it right. I'll get it right," he promised.

"I'm going to hate telling you goodbye later this

evening," she said. "But at least I'll be back in Knoxville for good in a couple of months."

"You don't have to tell me goodbye tonight. I called Director Pembrook and told her I needed a week of vacation. So, if you'll have me for the next seven days, I'll be here."

She laughed, and her eyes lit with the sparkle that he'd always loved. "Oh Evan, I'll definitely have you."

He pulled her back into his arms and kissed her once again, and in the kiss he knew he'd found his partner and his soulmate. This was one hostage situation he'd definitely gotten right for it had brought him back to the woman he loved.

* * * * *

Look for the next book in the
Tactical Crime Division *ensemble series—*
SECRET INVESTIGATION
by Elizabeth Heiter.

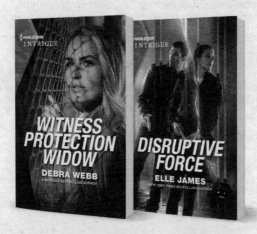

#1923 SECRET INVESTIGATION
Tactical Crime Division • by Elizabeth Heiter

When battle armor inexplicably fails and soldiers perish, the Tactical Crime Division springs into action. With the help of Petrov Armor CEO Leila Petrov, can undercover agent Davis Rogers discover secrets larger than anyone ever imagined?

#1924 CONARD COUNTY JUSTICE
Conard County: The Next Generation • by Rachel Lee

Major Daniel Duke will do whatever it takes to catch his brother's killer, but Deputy Cat Jansen is worried that he'll hinder her investigation. As the stakes increase, they must learn to work together to find the murderer. If they can't, they could pay with their lives...

#1925 WHAT SHE KNEW
Rushing Creek Crime Spree • by Barb Han

When a baby appears on navy SEAL Rylan Anderson's doorstep, he enlists old friend Amber Kent for help. But when the child is nearly abducted in Amber's care, they realize they must discover the truth behind the baby's identity in order to stop the people trying to kidnap her.

#1926 BACKCOUNTRY ESCAPE
A Badlands Cops Novel • by Nicole Helm

Felicity Harrison is being framed for murder. Family friend Gage Wyatt vows to keep her safe until they find the real culprit, but there's a killer out there who doesn't just want Felicity framed—but silenced for good.

#1927 THE HUNTING SEASON
by Janice Kay Johnson

After a string of murders connected to CPS social worker Lindsay Eagle's caseload is discovered, Detective Daniel Deperro is placed on protective detail. But Lindsay won't back down from the investigation, even as Daniel fears she's the next target. Will his twenty-four-hour protection enrage the killer further?

#1928 MURDER IN THE SHALLOWS
by Debbie Herbert

When a routine patrol sets Bailey Covington on the trail of a serial killer, the reclusive park ranger joins forces with sheriff's deputy Dylan Armstrong. Bailey can't forgive Dylan's family for betraying her, but they'll have to trust each other to find two missing women before a murderer strikes again.

YOU CAN FIND MORE INFORMATION ON UPCOMING HARLEQUIN TITLES, FREE EXCERPTS AND MORE AT HARLEQUIN.COM.

HICNM0420

She wiped up stray crumbs, then tried to smile at him.
"Coffee?"

"I've intruded too much."

She put a hand on her hip. "I might have thought
so earlier, but I'm not feeling that way now. This is
important. I give a damn about Larry, and now I give a
damn about you. You might not want it, but I care. So
quiet down. Coffee? Or something else?"

"A beer if you have another."

As it happened, she did. "I buy this so rarely that
you're in luck."

"Then why did you buy it?"

"Larry," she answered simply.

For the first time, they shared a look of real
understanding. The sense of connection warmed her.

She hadn't expected to feel this way, not when it came to Duke. Maybe it helped to realize he wasn't just a monolith of anger and unswaying determination.

As Cat returned to her seat, she said, "You put me off initially."

Another half smile from him. "I never would have guessed."

A laugh escaped her, brief but genuine. "I'm usually better at concealing my reactions to people. But there you were, looking like a battering ram. You sure looked hard and angry. Nothing about you made me want to get into a tussle."

He looked at the beer bottle he held. "Most people don't want to tangle with me. I can understand your reaction. I came through that door loaded for bear. Too much time to think on the way here, maybe."

"You looked like walking death," she told him frankly. "An icy-cold fury. Worse, in my opinion, than a heated rage. Scary."

"Comes with the territory," he said after a moment, then took a swig of his beer.

She could probably wonder until the cows came home exactly what he meant by that. Maybe it was better not to know.

Don't miss
Conard County Justice *by Rachel Lee,*
available May 2020 wherever
Harlequin Intrigue books and ebooks are sold.

Harlequin.com

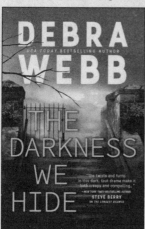

Winchester, Tennessee
Monday, March 9, 7:35 a.m.

Rowan Dupont parked on the southeast side of the downtown square. The county courthouse sat smack in the middle of Winchester with streets forming a grid around it. Shops, including a vintage movie theater, revitalized over the past few years by local artisans, lined the sidewalks. Something Rowan loved most about her hometown were the beautiful old trees that still stood above all else. So often the trees were the first things to go when towns received a face-lift. Not in Winchester. The entire square had been refreshed and the majestic old trees still stood.

This morning the promise of spring was impossible to miss. Blooms and leaves sprouted from every bare limb. This was her favorite time of year. A new beginning. Anything could happen.

Rowan sighed. Funny how being back in Winchester had come to mean so much to her these past several months. As a teenager she couldn't wait to get away from home. Growing up in a funeral home had made her different from the other kids. She was the daughter of the undertaker, a curiosity. At twelve tragedy had struck and she'd lost her twin sister and her mother within months of each other. The painful events had driven her to the very edge. By the time she'd finished high school, she was beyond ready for a change of scenery. Despite having spent more than twenty years living in the big city hiding from the memories of home and a dozen of those two decades working with Nashville's police department—in Homicide, no less—she had been forced to see that there was no running away. No hiding from the secrets of her past.

There were too many secrets, too many lies, to be ignored.

Yet despite all that had happened the first eighteen years of her life, she was immensely glad to be back home.

If only the most painful part of her time in Nashville— serial killer Julian Addington—hadn't followed her home and wreaked havoc those first months after her return.

Rowan took a breath and emerged from her SUV. The morning air was brisk and fresh. More glimpses of spring's impending arrival showed in pots overflowing with tulips, daffodils and crocuses. Those same early bloomers dotted the landscape beds all around the square. It was a new year and she was very grateful to have the previous year behind her.

She might not be able to change the past, but she could forge a different future, and she intended to do exactly that.

Don't miss
The Darkness We Hide *by Debra Webb,*
available April 2020 wherever
MIRA books and ebooks are sold.

Harlequin.com

MEXPDW947